A LOVE FOR ALL TIME

Men of Valor
Book One

By Laura Landon

ARE YOU SIGNED UP FOR DRAGONBLADE'S BLOG?

You'll get the latest news and information on exclusive giveaways, exclusive excerpts, coming releases, sales, free books, cover reveals and more.

Check out our complete list of authors, too!

No spam, no junk. That's a promise!

Sign Up Here

www.dragonbladepublishing.com

Dearest Reader;

Thank you for your support of a small press. At Dragonblade Publishing, we strive to bring you the highest quality Historical Romance from some of the best authors in the business. Without your support, there is no 'us', so we sincerely hope you adore these stories and find some new favorite authors along the way.

Happy Reading!

CEO, Dragonblade Publishing

CHAPTER ONE

London, England – Spring 1864

QUINTEN BECKHAM, EARL of Rosemont, decorated war hero and Colonel in Her Majesty's army, sat in a shadowed corner of The Ale and Pig and ordered another round of drinks for himself and his fellow officers—his most trusted friends.

"I'm sorry to hear about your brother and his wife, Colonel," Captain Theo Dunworthy said, after the barmaid set down their tankards of ale and walked away.

"Yes," Major Jackson Washburn added. "Their deaths were so tragic and unexpected. What are you going to do now?"

Quinn raked his fingers through his hair, then shook his head. "I don't know. The last thing I expected was to be saddled with a title and the responsibility of raising their two small children."

"What about the work we do for Her Majesty?" Theo whispered softly.

Quinn shook his head. "I can't imagine doing anything else. It's all I've ever wanted to do. It's all that makes my life worthwhile."

Theo leaned closer. "I know what you mean. I can't think of doing anything else either. I'm not sure I could."

The three friends looked at each other with sober expressions.

Quinn had been a spy for Her Majesty since the day he'd entered the army. There wasn't anything he could imagine doing that would give him more satisfaction than taking perilous risks to ensure England remained safe and secure.

"I'm facing one more problem," Quinn said, lifting his tankard and taking a hefty swallow.

He had his friends' full attention.

"I'm not sure how stable my brother left the estate. I checked the ledgers before I came to London, and it doesn't look good. I won't know until I meet with my solicitor in the morning. If things are bad, I may have to sell some of my properties. Either way, I'll probably have to take enough time away from government service to get things straightened out."

"Is there anything we can do to help you?" Theo asked and Quinn's heart swelled in his chest. God had blessed him with two of the best friends a man could ask for.

"I won't know until I meet with my solicitor."

"What about the mission Waterford already briefed us on?" Jack asked after taking a swallow of his ale.

"I promised I'd go, and I intend to keep my word. Besides, Waterford said it probably wouldn't take place for several weeks yet. That should give me time to settle my affairs and get my nieces taken care of."

"Is there anyone else who can look after the children?" Theo asked.

Quinn shook his head. "There was just my brother Robert and me."

"I don't envy you, Colonel," Jack said before finishing the ale in his tankard.

"You could always marry a rich wife," Theo quipped.

The three friends laughed.

"That's the last solution I'd entertain. Marriage is something none of us can consider in our line of work."

"That's surely true," Theo said, "but you have an advantage now. You're a decorated war hero, and titled. Finding a rich wife would solve any money problems you have. And, marrying would also solve finding someone to take care of your nieces."

"Getting married would also create more problems than it would ever solve, as well you know," Quinn said turning his gaze to Jack.

"Yes," Jack answered. "I know that all too well. Getting married is at the top of the list of the most stupid things I was ever foolish enough to do."

Although Quinn and Theo didn't know the details of what had happened to Jack's wife, they knew enough to realize his marriage had a tragic ending. And, whatever had happened, Jack still hadn't got over it.

Quinn finished the ale and set his tankard down on the table with a heavy thud. "Well, drinking more tonight won't solve any problems either, nor will it let me wake with a clear head tomorrow morning."

"No," Theo and Jack chorused as they slid back their chairs and rose.

They left the inn and walked down the street together, three companions whose friendship was forged in the most perilous of time and was still solidly in place.

There wasn't a more perilous time than the weeks and months during a war. The three friends had risked their lives more than once while fighting in Crimea. And each of them had come desperately close to dying.

Quinn remembered the time when he'd been captured behind enemy lines. He'd been wounded so severely while trying to escape he thought he wouldn't survive, but he was alive today because of his friends.

Theo and Jack refused to let him die. They came after him and helped him escape. And when he suffered a raging fever from his wounds, they sat at his bedside and demanded he stay alive. He was here today because of them. Nothing bonds a friendship closer. Quinn left them when he reached the Rosemont town house. He may as well make use of it while he still owned it. If things were as bad as he feared, the family town house would be the first property to be sold.

Quinn stumbled through the front door and up the stairs. He knew he would regret drinking as much as he had when he woke in the morning with a head that throbbed and he couldn't think straight. But the triple threat he faced had brought him low tonight.

Children, money, and marriage.

Of the three, there was only one he truly wished to solve. Money. For tonight he'd have to accept the fact that he was saddled with the first, woefully hopeless of finding the second, and determined to avoid even the merest hint of the third.

THE NEXT MORNING, plagued with the thundering headache he'd thoroughly expected to waken with, Quinten sat in solicitor Ira Young's musty office and stared at the shiny spot on the top of the elderly man's balding head. Young's thinning brown hair was turning gray and showed about as much life as the aging solicitor himself.

Quinn's chest grew tighter and tighter, pulsing in rhythm with his clenched jaw as he listened to the man.

"I'm truly sorry," the solicitor expressed with a genuine portrayal of true sorrow. "I wish I had better news for you, my lord, but…"

Quinn couldn't stand to be looked at with such a woeful expression of pity and rose to his feet. He walked on unsteady legs to the only window in the room and braced his hands on either side of the weathered window frame.

He didn't give a damn for *himself*. He'd always be able to take care of himself. But he had the children to think of now. What would happen to them?

"Please explain in detail everything I need to know. It's important that I am aware of exactly where I stand."

"Very well, my lord. But I'm afraid you will find it most distressing."

Quinn looked over his shoulder. "I survived a war, sir. I'm used to finding events distressing."

"Of course, my lord."

Quinn focused on the scene beyond the solicitor's window. A steady downpour of rain splattered against the glass panes making it difficult to clearly see the figures rushing for shelter.

"As you know, my lord, your brother—the former Earl of Rosemont—was not the best manager of what little your father passed down to him. His fondness for the gaming tables often emptied his pockets long before the estate's income had even been collected."

"Yes, Mr. Young. I'm aware of my late brother's shortcomings."

"Of course, my lord," the solicitor said as an apology. "But you see, everything that was left to him when your father died had been heavily borrowed against. Everything, of course, except the Rosemont estate, which is entailed."

"In other words, I will have to sell everything not entailed in order to cover the debts."

Ira Young cleared his throat. "Yes, except..." The solicitor cleared his throat a second time. "I'm afraid even if you were to sell all your properties not entailed, you would still be fearfully short of the amount you need to cover your debts."

"Bloody hell!" Quinn muttered. He slammed one fist against the window frame, then turned to face the solicitor.

The glass of brandy the man had poured Quinn when he'd first arrived drew Quinn back to the solicitor's desk. He drank the remainder of the liquor with an ungentlemanly gulp, then held the glass out when Ira Young extended the crystal decanter and offered him more.

"What options are left me?"

"I want you to know that I will help you as much as I can, but there's not much I can do. I warned your brother that he was perilously close to losing everything. I'm afraid he was of the opinion that in time his luck would change and he'd be able to satisfy all his debtors."

"But of course, his luck didn't change."

"No. I must say that it was with a terribly heavy heart that I had to inform you of his and his wife's deaths."

Quinn remembered the letter he'd received informing him that Robert had been killed in a carriage accident. And that Robert's wife Elaine, upon hearing the news, had gone into labor with their second child and died in childbirth. It seemed a mixed mercy that the child had survived only to become his ward. He knew nothing about children, especially the care of a babe so young. Just as he knew he would make a most inept guardian.

"Lord Rosemont," the solicitor said, pulling Quinn from his thoughts.

It took Quinn a moment to realize the solicitor was speaking to him. He still wasn't accustomed to being addressed as the Earl of Rosemont. It was a title he'd never expected to carry. Robert was always so healthy and robust. It never occurred to Quinn that anything could bring down his brother. But now a temperamental carriage horse had left Quinn with responsibilities he could never have anticipated. And didn't want.

"You asked what options were open to you. There is, of course, marriage. You—"

"No. Marriage is *not* an option."

"But, the children—"

"No!" Quinn raked his fingers through his thick, dark hair. "What other options are there?"

Mr. Young shuffled through the papers on his desk and shook his head. "For now, I suggest that you take this list of all your brother's creditors. I will make up a list of all the properties in the Rosemont name and obtain a possible sale price we can expect from each property. Then we will set forth a plan to sell the properties and pay off the most pressing creditors first. It's the only way we'll know what remains of the estate." He coughed slightly. "If indeed there's anything left."

Quinn let the magnitude of what he'd have to do settle over him. This meant he'd lose Willowbrook Manor, the estate his mother had brought to her marriage. It was the place Quinn had gone to with his mother when she wanted to escape the hustle and chaos of London life. She disliked the City during the crush of the Season as much as Quinn did, and sought refuge at Willowbrook. Some of the best days of his life had taken place in the country with his mother.

It would kill him if he was forced to give up Willowbrook Manor. It was the place where he could roam freely. Where he'd learned to fish and shoot, and use a bow and arrow. Where he'd learned to ride and become proficient with a rifle. Where he could avoid the heavy hand of his father and learn the gentler side of human nature from his mother.

Quinn raked his fingers through his hair and came to grips with everything he would lose. A heavy weight settled against his chest. For the first time in his life he disliked his brother. Oh, he'd been angry with him more times than he could count, but he'd never disliked him. Now, his anger was more heated than ever before. Almost to the point of hatred.

"Are there any other questions, my lord?" Ira Young asked.

There was sympathy in the solicitor's eyes, compassion in his voice. Quinn hated that. He'd never felt like such a failure in his life and that wasn't an emotion he wanted to acknowledge.

"No, Mr. Young. Give me the bloody list."

"As you wish," the solicitor said, then rose to offer the list and shake Quinn's hand.

Quinn's legs threatened to buckle beneath him as he left the well-appointed office that reeked of success and walked to where he'd left his horse. He threw a coin to the lad he'd asked to watch Atlas and put his foot in the stirrup. He'd best be careful with his coin now. The very thought made him wince.

Images of tenant cottages and carriage horses and elegant

furnishings and precious china that were about to disappear from his holdings paraded through his mind. With them he could turn the head of any number of wealthy young women into eager brides. Without them? Quinn prayed he could at least manage to keep possession of his mother's favorites.

Quinn turned Atlas into the avenue. The last thing he cared about was an eager bride.

CHAPTER TWO

*H*OW THE HELL *was he going to survive this?* Quinn asked himself as he mounted his horse. He knew Robert had spent more than the estate was capable of earning, but he never considered that his brother would risk everything for a game of cards. He was more responsible than that. At least, Quinn had thought he was.

Quinn stopped at his club and ordered a bottle of brandy. He drank one glass of the fine liquor, then another. He hoped drinking enough of the mind-numbing liquid would dull his disillusionment and force the disastrous news he'd heard today to evaporate. Or perhaps when he woke he could pretend for at least a few hours that what he'd learned today had been a drunken delusion.

But he knew that was impossible.

Quinn drained the liquor in his glass, then rose from his table and left. It wouldn't do any good to put off what he had to do. His brother's debtors weren't going to go away. And his debts weren't going to magically get paid no matter how much he drank to forget his troubles.

Quinn staggered slightly as he made his way to the mews behind the club and mounted Atlas. He didn't think he'd had so much to drink that he was drunk, but maybe the shock of the news he'd learned today as well as a lack of food caused the liquor to affect him more than usual.

He rode through the streets at a faster pace than was safe. Thankfully, because of the pouring rain, most pedestrians had already gone home or had taken shelter from the downpour, and the streets were fairly empty.

As dusk approached, the rain worsened, assaulting him with stinging drops laced with sleet. It was difficult for Quinn to see even several yards ahead.

He considered going home to Rosemont Hall tonight, but had enough common sense to realize the roads weren't safe enough for Atlas. He may as well stay in Town. The Rosemont townhouse would no doubt be the first to go on the auction block.

Quinn pictured the palatial townhouse in the fashionable part of London. *I should use it while I still have it. The day will come when I don't have it any longer.*

Another blast of wind pelted rain across his face, momentarily making it impossible to see. Atlas slipped on the rain-soaked slick cobbles and Quinn reacted swiftly to get him under control. The last thing he wanted was for his prize horse to be injured.

Quinn pulled on the reins, but Atlas refused to calm. He reared on his hind legs and whinnied in fright, prancing from side to side. A bolt of lightning struck close by and Atlas raced ahead a few yards, then reared again.

Quinn wasn't sure what he heard first: Atlas's alarmed whinny or a woman's terrified scream.

In one terrible instant, Atlas reared again, and the scream was cut short.

Quinn knew what had happened. He had just run someone down.

He wheeled around in the saddle. A well-dressed woman lay in the street, undoubtedly injured. Or perhaps dead. Her gloved hand trailed out from her side. A petite, still hand. Too still.

Quinn leaped to the ground and raced back to where the woman lay in a heap on the cobbles. She was small, fragile.

Helpless. Quinn sank to his knees beside her and turned her into his arms.

He didn't recognize her and looked about in bewilderment, searching for anyone who might know who she was. He had no choice but to help her. Even though he didn't want to get involved, he felt a protectiveness toward her he hadn't felt for anyone since the years he'd spent in the war This was the same emotion that had consumed him whenever he came upon a young soldier who'd been severely injured. A lad too young to be called a man. A lad who would never live to become a man.

Most of the soldiers under his command were barely old enough to be there. They were hardly old enough to be out of the schoolroom and here they were, thrown into battle where they were forced to see the worst part of humanity. Where they saw and experienced the horrors of war that caused even seasoned soldiers to have nightmares. When he came upon a young soldier who no doubt wouldn't live to see tomorrow, he was compelled to do whatever he could to console the lad until he took his last breath.

Quinn felt the same about the young woman in his arms, a protectiveness that was similar to how he'd felt during the war, yet different. The woman in his arms wasn't a soldier. She wasn't a young lad. She was a woman, and the emotions rushing through him were totally alien from any emotions he'd ever felt.

Totally alien from any emotions he wanted to feel. Especially for an unknown woman.

At that moment, a footman from one of the nearby townhouses ran toward him.

"Do you recognize her?" Quinn yelled.

"It's hard to say, my lord," the servant answered, and only then did Quinn realize that the woman was so disheveled that it *was* hard to tell who she might be. Her hair was plastered across her face, making her unrecognizable. Blood ran from a gash in her forehead, streaking what could be seen of her visage.

Quinn reached for his handkerchief and wiped gently across

her cheek.

"Dear lord," the man beside him said in an emotional voice.

"Do you know her?"

"Yes, my lord. It's Lady Cassandra."

"Does she live nearby?"

"Yes, my lord. Right here," the man said, pointing to the townhouse in the center of the block. "She's the Dowager Countess of Granville's granddaughter."

"Go to the door and tell them what's happened, and ask them to send for a doctor. I'm going to carry the lady inside."

"Yes, my lord. Right away, my lord," the man said, then ran to do as he was ordered.

Quinn gently lifted the lady into his arms and held her for a moment. He felt a pull towards her that was totally alien from any emotion he'd ever felt before, a protectiveness he wasn't used to feeling.

She was injured because of him. He was the cause of her injuries. Even though he didn't want to feel a responsibility toward her, he did. Just like he'd felt responsible for every soldier under his command.

He nestled her closer, shielding her from the pouring rain. She moaned in pain no matter how careful he tried to be. It was difficult, though. She was injured badly, and he needed to get her inside as soon as possible. As he stepped toward the house, one of Lady Granville's hall boys appeared to take charge of Atlas.

Quinn carried Lady Cassandra across the street and through the door another of the dowager countess's house staff held open for him.

"Show me to this lady's room," he ordered the butler who stood wringing his hands in the front hall.

A maid rushed ahead of him to lead the way up the staircase.

"Has anyone gone for a doctor?"

"Yes, my lord," the butler answered as he followed Quinn upwards. "He should be here soon."

"Good," Quinn answered, then placed the lady on the bed the

maid indicated. "Bring warm water and clean cloths. And bring the lady some dry clothes."

"Yes, my lord," the butler answered, then issued orders to the staff. Several servants rushed from the room.

Quinn let his gaze peruse the still figure before him. This wasn't the first time he'd seen an injured body, but this was the first time he'd felt such a reaction to what he saw. Whether that was because he was the cause of those injuries, or the injured person was a woman, he didn't know, but his reaction was all-consuming.

His hand reached out and touched her face, caressed her cheek.

"Is Cassandra alive?" a commanding voice asked from the doorway and Quinn pulled back his hand.

He lifted his head and locked gazes with a dignified, elderly woman. Without being introduced, he knew she must be the Dowager Countess of Granville.

"Yes, my lady. She's alive. But she's been severely injured."

The dowager countess crossed the room with the same regal aplomb that Quinn was accustomed to seeing from his commanding officers. He was impressed with her refusal to exhibit any hint of alarm, even though concern was evident in her gaze.

"I'm afraid the fault is mine, my lady. I struck her with my horse."

"And you are?"

"Quinten Beckham, Earl of Rosemont, my lady."

Quinn returned his attention to the woman on the bed. He took a warm cloth from one of the maids, and gently wiped the lady's face. The paleness he revealed was so shocking that it set his fingers shaking as he carefully loosened the uppermost button of her gown at the neck. It was paramount, he felt certain, to help the lady breathe more freely. He was compelled to loosen the lady's gown further, as well, but would not do so under the forbidding gaze of the dowager countess. He did, however, run his hands atop her clothing down the length of her legs, stopping only when his fingers reached the turn of her slender ankles.

"No discernible broken bones, my lady."

"Excuse me, Lord Rosemont," the dowager countess said rather stiffly, "but are you a doctor?"

"No, my lady. I've not been formally trained. But during the war in Crimea, I assisted army doctors with the wounded. With your permission, I could staunch as much of your granddaughter's bleeding as possible before the doctor arrives."

"Then by all means do so, my lord," the dowager countess said as she stepped closer to her granddaughter. "Is there anything I can do to help?"

"If you or one of your maids would remove your granddaughter's shoes and stockings, that would be helpful. I must stop the bleeding here," Quinn said, pressing down on a nasty slash on the lady's shoulder. It looked as though Atlas's hoof had torn her flesh. It was going to take several stitches from the doctor to close the wound.

Quinn caught a glimpse of another bloody place on the lady's back and tried to move her enough to see how badly she was injured there, but when he turned her, she moaned in pain.

"I'm sorry, my lady," Quinn said. "I don't mean to cause you more pain, but I need to see how badly you're injured."

When the two maids had removed Lady Cassandra's shoes and stockings, the dowager countess came to the head of the bed. "Tell me what to do." An unmistakable note of urgent concern had crept into the regal woman's voice.

"If you're able, you could hold a cloth on that wound on her forehead."

"Of course," the dowager countess said. She swiftly rinsed a cloth in fresh water and began working to keep the blood from flowing into her granddaughter's eyes.

The young lady had several cuts and bruises on her face. As the dowager countess wiped more and more of the mud and blood away, Quinn got his first look at the woman before him.

It was impossible to assess the woman's comeliness with so

many cuts and bruises marring Lady Cassandra's features. But he could tell that she was not terribly young. If Quinn had to guess, he'd estimate she was nearing her thirtieth year. Perhaps she was even closer to his own thirty and three.

He didn't know what color her eyes were. She had yet to open them. And he doubted she would be able to for a day or two, considering how swollen and bruised her face was becoming.

Her lips might be luscious and full, but it was hard to say how much of their fullness was a result of the swelling around her cheeks and mouth, and how much was natural.

Quinn lifted a cloth for one of the servants to rinse when the door opened, and the doctor entered. A woman followed on the man's heels. An assistant, Quinn thought, and he was glad.

"What do we have here, my lady?" the doctor asked the dowager countess.

"It's Lady Cassandra. She and Lord Rosemont collided in the street. It was raining, as you know, and Cassie ran in front of Lord Rosemont's horse."

The doctor removed his coat and rolled up his sleeves, then began to examine his patient. He'd only taken a glance at some of Lady Cassandra's injuries before he spoke. "Lady Granville, why don't you and Lord Rosemont retire downstairs and have a cup of tea while Mrs. Dampers and I see to your granddaughter. The staff can go, too. Except for one of the women."

"You will let me know how my granddaughter is as soon as you discover the extent of her injuries," the dowager countess said, more as a statement than a question.

"Of course, my lady," the doctor answered.

Quinn stepped away from the bed, then escorted Lady Granville from the room. The second he stepped into the hallway, his legs threatened to give out beneath him. He reached for the banister that overlooked the foyer below and braced his outstretched arms on the polished wooden railing.

For a moment he thought he might be ill. As if in a nightmare, the scene of the moment Atlas's hooves came down atop the woman crossing the street flashed in his mind. He gripped the railing tighter.

He'd nearly killed an innocent woman. If only he hadn't been in such an angry rush to leave London. If only he hadn't had so much to drink. If only he had been watching more carefully.

If only this hadn't already been such a hell of a day.

Quinn lowered his head between his outstretched arms. What if the lady he'd trampled died? What if her injuries were so extensive she did not survive? Or she suffered some permanent injuries that scarred her for life?

"Lord Rosemont?"

Quinn turned to see Lady Granville standing beside him. She was the epitome of stateliness. She held her composure as if she were hosting an event at which calmness and elegance were required.

Quinn estimated that the dowager countess had reached her seventieth year, but she looked far from her age. She held herself with all the distinction he was accustomed to seeing in the nobility.

"Would you please escort me down? I've ordered tea, but I think you and I might require something stronger. Am I correct?"

"Yes, my lady," Quinn said extending his arm.

The dowager countess placed her hand on his forearm and Quinn led her down and into a beautiful drawing room.

Quinn took the glass of brandy Lady Granville's butler poured for him and carried it to the window next to where the dowager countess sat in a finely upholstered cushioned chair. He owed the dowager an explanation, as well as an apology. Yet, the words were difficult to organize. Quinn was surprised when she spoke first.

"I want you to know that I don't blame you for the accident, Lord Rosemont."

"But you should, my lady. The accident was my fault. I was going too fast—"

"As I'm sure Cassie was, too. It was pouring down rain and you were both in a hurry to get to shelter."

Quinn turned. How could she be so understanding?

"I should have looked more carefully."

"Cassie should have, too."

Quinn carried his glass of brandy to the chair next to the dowager and sat. "How can you be so understanding, my lady?"

"Let me ask you a question, my lord. If you could have avoided the accident, would you have?"

Quinn was shocked. "Of course. I would never intentionally—"

Lady Granville held up her hand to stop him from finishing. She lifted the crystal decanter the butler had left on a tray on the table next to the dowager's chair and handed it to Quinn. He filled his empty glass, then added a generous amount to Lady Granville's glass.

"Let me tell you a story. When I was a young girl, no more than thirteen or fourteen, I did something quite similar to what happened to you today. Only, it involved my sister." Lady Granville stopped to take a sip of her brandy.

"I had been gifted a pony for my birthday. It wasn't a fast pony, but was perfect for pulling a small wagon my father kept in the stables. I drove it up and down the lane on our estate from morning to dusk." She stopped herself and huffed. "Well, at least until the pony refused to go any further."

She smiled.

"I loved to drive the wagon and often went too fast, just as you were going today."

She paused as if remembering that day. "My sister Sarah constantly asked to go along, but I always refused to take her. She was younger by three years and was very brave until the wagon started moving. Then she would become frightened and beg me to stop and take her back to the house. As you might guess, one day I tired of her begging and thought to teach her a lesson. I let her ride with me. We'd barely started moving when she cried that she wanted to get off. But I refused to stop. I even pushed my pony to go faster."

Lady Granville took another sip of her liquor. "I drove down the lane, then made a circle to go back. I must have taken the circle too fast, and Sarah fell off the wagon and broke her leg."

The dowager countess locked her gaze with his. "Was the accident my fault? Of course it was. Do I wish I could go back and relive that day and prevent the accident from happening? Of course I do. But we aren't able to turn back the clock at our convenience. We live with what we've done and try not to repeat our errors."

Quinn stared at the dowager countess's face. Her refusal to condemn him as he condemned himself moved him greatly.

"May I ask you a question, my lord?"

"Of course, my lady."

"Why did you make the effort to stop to see to my grand-daughter?"

Quinn looked at the dowager countess in surprise. "How could I not, my lady?"

"Surely you realize there are many who would not have bothered to stop."

Quinn paused before he could answer. "Perhaps not, my lady. But I am not one of those. I have seen enough death to know how precious life is."

"Yes, I don't doubt you have, my lord. Nor do I doubt that you would like to relive some of the battles you fought during the war and change the outcome. But that is not possible, is it?"

"No, my lady. It is not possible.

"Just as it is not possible to change what happened today. The fault was not yours, my lord. Just as it was not Cassandra's. Never think that either of you were to blame."

Quinn sat in awe of this forgiving woman. He wouldn't have blamed her if she'd had him thrown out of her house. He wouldn't have blamed her if she had him brought up on charges. Instead, she tried her hardest to help Quinn forgive himself.

"You are quite remarkable, my lady. I cannot thank you enough for your kindness."

A knock sounded at the door before she could respond, and the doctor entered the room.

"How is my granddaughter?"

"She took quite a blow to her head as well as several severe cuts and bruises, but she will be fine in time. She needs plenty of quiet and rest."

"Which I will make sure she gets," the dowager countess assured the doctor.

"I know you will, my lady. And, how are you faring?"

The dowager countess paused for a moment, then graced the doctor with a sad smile. "Well, Dr. Hector. As well as can be expected."

"Converse," the dowager countess said as she turned to her butler. "Please pay Dr. Hector, then take him to the kitchen. I think Cook was just taking some biscuits out of the oven."

The doctor smiled. "Thank you, Lady Granville. Call if you need anything. If not, I'll call on you again in the morning."

Lady Granville bid the doctor farewell, then turned to Quinn. "I know you are anxious to return home. Could I ask you a favor before you leave?"

"Of course, my lady."

"Would you escort me up to sit with my granddaughter? I find it difficult to manage the stairs alone."

"It would be my pleasure."

Quinn rose and helped the dowager countess to her feet. She leaned more heavily on him than she had earlier. The stress of the day had begun to take its toll on her. When they reached the stairs, her steps were even more labored as she leaned on his arm.

Quinn remembered the doctor asking her how she was faring. He also remembered her answer. *As well as can be expected.*

He focused on Lady Granville when he ushered her into her granddaughter's room. He pushed a chair forward so she could sit next to her granddaughter's bed. Her face had lost much of its earlier color and her hands visibly shook in her lap.

Quinn turned his attention from grandmother to granddaughter. The lady lying on the bed seemed to be resting comfortably, but Quinn was sure that was because the doctor had given her enough laudanum to allow her to sleep for several hours.

The cuts and bruises he'd seen earlier now seemed darker and angrier. He knew she would be in a great deal of pain for several days. But at least she was alive. He didn't have the lady's death on his conscience.

Lady Granville lifted her gaze. "Thank you for your assistance, my lord. I'm sure you have many things that require your attention, so I won't force you to stay any longer."

"It's not an imposition, my lady. It's the least I can do."

Lady Granville extended her hand and Quinn took it, then lifted it to his lips.

"Go now, my lord. I'll be in touch with you soon."

Quinn nodded, then turned to leave. At the doorway he turned back to take a final look at the lady he'd nearly killed this afternoon. Somehow, he felt responsible for what had happened to her. He knew the dowager countess didn't hold him responsible, and if he had to dig deep beneath the surface, he wouldn't be able to explain why he felt responsible for her injuries.

Quinn left the room, thinking he'd more than likely never see the woman again. But he would never forget the sight of her broken body lying in the middle of the street.

Nearly two weeks had gone by since the fateful day when his horse had struck Lady Cassandra Walsh. Quinn couldn't forget her torn and bruised body.

He hadn't heard anything from Lady Granville and prayed that no news was good news. He couldn't get the lady out of his mind and prayed she was healing. He didn't want to think that she was still in such pain. Or, that she'd come down with a fever. Suffering a fever was fatal, more times than not.

Quinn was sitting at the breakfast table with a heaping plate of coddled eggs before him. Before he finished his food, his butler entered the room.

"A message, my lord," his butler announced, carrying a folded note on a silver tray.

"Thank you, Rievers." Quinn took the message from the tray and stared at it. The message was from the Dowager Countess of Granville.

Quinn's heart stuttered in his chest. He doubted the message held good news.

Quinn opened the missive and read it. It was short and contained no pleasantries.

Please come see me at your earliest convenience.

Lady Granville.

"Bad news, my lord?" Rievers asked.

"I don't know. Have Atlas saddled and brought round to the front, Rievers."

"Yes, my lord," his butler answered, as he left the room.

Quinn didn't want to speak his thoughts out loud, but they refused to go away. Why else would the Dowager Countess of Granville need to see him?

Unless the woman he struck had not survived.

CHAPTER THREE

QUINN ARRIVED AT the Dowager Countess of Granville's townhouse less than an hour later. It had been the longest ride he'd ever endured. He dreaded looking into Lady Granville's face when she broke the news that her granddaughter was dead. He dreaded knowing that he was responsible for another human being's death.

He'd been responsible for so many deaths during the war. He'd watched so many young men die from wounds he'd inflicted. Watched so many fellow soldiers die from wounds he couldn't save them from. His chest ached with a pain that would not go away. Now, he was to endure that pain yet again.

He walked up the short walk, then entered the house when the butler he'd met two weeks earlier opened the door.

"Lord Rosemont," the butler greeted with a regal bow. "Please," he said pointing down a long hallway. "Lady Granville will see you in the morning room."

Quinn followed the butler who led him to a bright, sunny room.

Quinn was surprised. He didn't expect that the windows of the house would be so open. And now that he recalled, there was no black ribbon or wreath on the outside door, nor was straw spread on the street outside to muffle the noise of passing carriages.

Could it be that there hadn't been a death at Lady Granville's townhouse? That her granddaughter wasn't dead?

Quinn entered the room and found Lady Granville sitting in a chair near the fireplace.

"Please, come in," she said. "Forgive me for not rising, but the rainy weather we've had over the past few days is not kind to my bones."

"That is understandable," Quinn said.

He followed the butler to a chair, then accepted a cup of tea when a maid offered him one. It was evident that her ladyship's aching bones kept her from handling the tea service herself. When the servants finished, they quit the room and Quinn and Lady Granville were left alone.

"I'm sure you wonder why I've asked to see you," she said.

"I'd be lying if I said I didn't. I would first like to ask after your granddaughter. Has she regained consciousness?"

"Thankfully, yes. She is still in a certain amount of pain, but that's to be expected."

"Yes. I wish her a speedy recovery. Pain is not something anyone wishes on another person."

"A condition on which you have a certain amount of knowledge, I would imagine," the dowager countess added.

Quinn raised his eyebrows. He wondered how the dowager countess knew this and he couldn't hide his confusion.

Lady Granville smiled. "I would like to explain my reason for asking to speak with you, but before I do, I would ask that you keep our conversation in the strictest confidence. As I promise to do the same."

She locked her gaze with Quinn's and waited until he gave her his word.

"Of course, my lady. Nothing you say will leave these four walls."

She nodded in response. "I beg that you do not take offense at my forwardness, but I have become acquainted with certain aspects of your personal life."

"How, may I ask, did such acquaintance transpire?" Quinn felt uneasy. Had the woman had him investigated?

"Oh yes. Well, of course you would wish to know."

Quinn observed the tiniest squirm before the dowager continued.

"You see, my granddaughter's second cousin called on us to wish her a speedy recovery, and by happenstance he is acquainted with you. Professionally, of course."

Quinn blinked. "And this second cousin is…?"

"He is a solicitor, my lord. Ira Young, Esquire."

Quinn lifted his eyebrows, and placed his cup of tea on the table beside his chair. He suddenly wished his cup contained something stronger. "And did he share anything you didn't know before?"

She coughed gracefully. "As it happens, he did. For instance, I discovered that you are a highly decorated war hero."

"As were many other officers in Her Majesty's service."

"But few were given the outstanding medals you were awarded."

Quinn couldn't find the words he wanted to say. He never thought he deserved the accolades he received. Those should have gone to the soldiers that laid down their lives for their country.

"I also discovered that you never envied your brother his title."

"No, my lady. I was only forced to assume the Rosemont title when my brother died in an incident on the road."

"And your sister-in-law died in childbirth shortly after your brother. You have since been ward of your two nieces, one nearing five years and the other barely five months."

"I congratulate you, my lady. Your investigative research has been quite accurate. And extensive."

"Then you will not be surprised when I tell you that I discovered you are still in Her Majesty's service. In a highly secretive capacity."

Quinn couldn't hide his surprise. He sat upright and pressed against the back of the chair.

"Ira did not divulge that to me, I assure you, sir. I have a friend in high places in government who supplied that delicate bit of information when I sought to confirm Ira's revelations."

"I see."

"And finally, I know you are on the brink of bankruptcy."

At last Quinn exhaled. "Ah, yes. I wondered when you would get to that point."

The dowager countess lifted her cup of tea and took a swallow. When she set it back down, she locked her serious gaze with his. "I'm not sure if you are aware or not, but I am a very wealthy woman."

Quinn didn't respond to her statement. Instead he stretched his long, muscular legs out in front of him. He thought of any number of suggestions the dowager countess intended to make. There must be some point to informing him that she was wealthy.

Perhaps she needed something from him. Something to do with his position in the government. If she knew he worked in a highly secretive capacity, she also assumed he had secret information at his disposal. Perhaps she needed someone investigated. Quinn wondered how he could refuse her request without offending her.

Quinn couldn't imagine anything else the dowager countess might need from him. By her own account, she was a very wealthy woman, and he was on the brink of bankruptcy. So, money had nothing to do with whatever she needed from him.

He didn't speak, but waited for the dowager countess to get to the point she intended. Except when she did, her words were not what he expected.

"I am not a young woman, Lord Rosemont. And, because of some health issues, I don't have long to live. A month or two, perhaps. Or less. So I'm told."

Quinn pulled his legs beneath him and sat straighter. "I'm

sorry to hear it, my lady."

A sad smile lifted the corners of her mouth. "Do not pity me. I have had a long and very enjoyable life."

"Does your granddaughter know you are ill?"

Lady Granville shook her head. "Nor do I want her to until it's absolutely necessary. It would only complicate matters."

"What matters are those?"

"I have an offer I would like you to consider. Please, consider my words before you reject what I am about to suggest."

Quinn raised his eyebrows. "You anticipate that I may refuse your offer?"

"The possibility crossed my mind. One of the traits I discovered about you is your independence, as well as your pride."

"Do you consider those negative traits?"

"That is yet to be seen."

"I see," Quinn said, then clenched his hands around the arms of the chair in preparation for the lady's proposition.

"I am offering to pay your creditors in full, my lord, and provide you with enough money that you will not lack for funds in the foreseeable future."

Quinn was unable to breathe. He rose from his chair and walked to one of the multi-paned windows that overlooked the street in front of Lady Granville's townhouse. The street was not busy, but several carriages passed by before he looked away.

"I could not possibly accept, my lady."

"I thought as much, my lord, which is why I have already instructed Ira to draw up the appropriate papers to ensure I achieve my intended goal. You see, out of my compassion for two orphaned children, I am settling their father's debts and seeking to ensure their future welfare. To that end, I am putting in place a trust for each child and a stipend for their ward which can only be considered extremely… generous."

Quinn turned his head and stared in disbelief as the elegant woman tilted her head to spear him with a gaze from which he dared not look away.

"There is but one condition."

And that is what had been lurking behind her gaze, he realized. There was a condition attached to her generosity which he doubted very much he could tolerate.

"And what, may I ask, might this condition entail?"

"I expect you to marry my granddaughter."

Quinn turned to face the dowager countess. "You what?"

"I expect you to marry my granddaughter."

Bloody hell. She was serious. She truly expected him to marry a woman he'd never met before. A woman he'd nearly killed.

He turned to look back out the window, although his mind was spinning in such turmoil he didn't notice anything that was going on outside.

No, he couldn't do it. Even knowing every one of his debts would be paid and he wouldn't lose any of the properties he owned. He couldn't do it. He could never marry. Marriage would mean he would have to give up working for Her Majesty. Marriage would mean he would have to spend the rest of his life caring for the tenants who farmed his land. Deciding what crops were planted when and where. Deciding how many cows and sheep each tenant would raise.

Quinn couldn't imagine anything more boring. The most excitement he'd ever have would be balancing farming ledgers. If that was all there was to life, he was certain he would go stark, raving mad in less than a year.

He braced his hands on either side of the window and lowered his head between his outstretched arms.

"I'm sorry, my lady," he said without turning to face her. "But I'm afraid that is impossible. It isn't that I doubt your granddaughter would make an admirable wife. The fault for a disastrous marriage would be completely mine. I am unable to make *any* woman an acceptable husband. The work I do is too important for me to give it up to be a husband."

Quinn straightened his stance but still did not turn to face her. "And," he continued after clearing his throat, "the assignments on which I'm sent are often considered dangerous."

"Your point being?" she asked.

He turned to address her from a commanding stance. "My point being that it is highly likely that I may not survive one of these assignments. If that were to occur, I would leave your granddaughter a widow before she has hardly been a wife. Not only would she be left with an estate to run, but two small girls to raise."

Once the words were out Quinn felt the honesty of his statement and prayed she would feel it, too. But when she spoke, he discovered she intended to press for his agreement.

"So you would impoverish yourself and the children with you."

He felt the air leave his body. It was difficult to maintain any poise after her shattering words—*you would impoverish yourself and the children too.*

"I see that the specter of poverty alarms you, my lord, as well it should, so let me explain the qualities I require in a husband for my granddaughter. Please, do come sit."

Quinn returned to his chair next to Lady Granville. It didn't take her long to get to the point of why she'd sent for him.

"I am looking for a man who will never mistreat my granddaughter. Can you assure me that you are not a violent man?"

Quinn was taken aback by Lady Granville's first requirement. "I would never strike a woman, my lady. I would never intentionally cause her physical or emotional harm."

She nodded her agreement. "I am also looking for a man who will provide for, and care for, my granddaughter, as well as provide her with a certain amount of companionship."

"I would never allow her to lack anything she is used to having, but affection is not—"

The Dowager Countess of Granville held up her hand to halt Quinn's words. "I do not expect you to fall in love with my granddaughter, although I hope you find her so exceptional that in time you will."

Quinn shook his head. "I cannot fathom that there would be love between us," he answered.

"Then I will leave the possibility of that to God."

Quinn waited a few moments in silence. "I cannot give up the work I do for Her Majesty, my lady. It is too vital. Too important."

"What if I told you I don't expect you to give up the work you do? Accepting what you do will be a concession my granddaughter will have to make."

Lady Granville pointed to a side table against the opposite wall. "I'm sure you'd like something stronger than a tepid cup of tea while I explain the reason for my offer. Please, pour me a glass of wine, and help yourself to what you would prefer."

Quinn rose from his chair and poured the dowager a glass of wine and himself a glass of brandy. He wanted to down the entire glass in one swallow, but thought better of it. He took both glasses and returned to his chair. When he handed the dowager countess her wine, he sat.

"I'm sure you are aware of how different men can be. Even brothers. So it was with my children." Lady Granville paused long enough to take a sip of her wine. "Cassandra's father, Winston, was my oldest. He inherited the title Earl of Granville from my husband when he died, and my dear husband would have been very proud of how Winston conducted himself and ran the estates he was given. But not all my sons had Winston's abilities. When Winston died, the earldom passed to my second son, Gerald."

Lady Granville's face took on a sad expression and Quinn knew she was not going to say as admirable things about her second son as she'd spoken about her oldest son.

"Gerald did not have Winston's keen business mind. Nor was he as reliable or dependable. He enjoyed London's nightlife far too much and spent too much time at the gaming tables. My husband had to pay his debts more than once when Gerald was a young man and found himself in too deep, and even Winston came to his brother's aid when he overspent his allowance."

Lady Granville took another sip of her wine, then locked her gaze with Quinn's. "As a mother, I am not proud to say that Gerald also had a hot temper that got him into more fights than I'd like to admit."

"And he hasn't changed since he's become earl?" Quinn asked.

"No. If anything, he's become worse. That is why I'm desperate to find a husband for Cassandra."

"She is a beautiful woman. I would think she'd have married by now."

"She nearly was," the dowager said. "She was betrothed several years ago to the Marquess of Weatherly. But it ended badly."

"What happened?"

"The earl left her at the altar and eloped with his childhood sweetheart. It broke Cassandra's heart. She swore she would never marry."

"I'm afraid I don't understand," Quinn said. "Why is it so important for you to force her to marry if she doesn't wish to marry?"

"Because of her uncle, my lord. The current Earl of Granville is going through money like the well will never run dry, and when he becomes desperate for enough money to pay his creditors, he'll look to Cassandra and the trust she will inherit. I fear he'll either force her to marry someone who promises to pay him an astronomical amount for her hand, or he'll force her to turn her dowry over to him. Cassandra will not be safe until she is married to someone I can trust."

"And you think that *someone* is me?"

"Yes, Colonel. That someone is you."

"You realize our marriage will probably never include the love she might wish for, don't you, my lady?"

Lady Granville focused her gaze on Quinn. "Colonel, I have no intention of forcing my granddaughter into a marriage devoid of love and affection. It is my hope, as well as my most sincere desire that in time you and Cassie will come to love and care for each other as desperately as any couple who marries for love. My desire is that, in time, her husband will love and care for her. And it's important that I find that person while I am still alive.

Quinn rose from his chair and walked to the window. He had much to think about, much to consider.

"Now, is there anything else you'd like clarified?"

Quinn turned. "What if your granddaughter refuses to go along with your plan?"

"Convincing her will be my responsibility." The dowager countess waited a short time before she continued. "My granddaughter is an intelligent individual. I have every confidence that in time she will realize my plan is the wisest course of action. Indeed, the *only* way to thwart Gerald's manipulations."

Quinn was speechless. He had no idea what answer he should give the dowager countess. She was offering him the answer to all his problems. Safety and security for his nieces. A way to save his estate, as well as Willowbrook Manor. The ability to continue his work with the government while at the same time providing a mother for Lizzy and Molly.

"I know my offer was quite unexpected. Just as I know the care and wellbeing of your two nieces weighs heavily upon you. The money I am offering you will alleviate that concern and allow you to raise the children in the style in which they should be reared. And, I am certain that Cassie would be a positive influence on the girls and give them love and attention."

There wasn't another fact that the dowager countess could recite that would push Quinn toward the choice he had to make. The care of Lizzy and Molly was paramount. He wasn't prepared to be a father to the two small children, let alone both mother and father. He required help, and Lady Cassandra could fill that role perfectly. And with his financial burden relieved, he could secure additional employees to aid Cassandra in the nursery.

Quinn finished his brandy. "I need time to consider your

offer, my lady. Will you give me a few days to think about all this?"

"Of course, my lord. I don't intend to die in the next few days. But—" She lowered her voice. "I'm sure I do not need to point out to you that the greater gift in all this is to me—knowing that my granddaughter is safe from my son, and that her future is secure."

A tear slid from the dear lady's eye and she made no effort to swipe it away. As it slipped down her cheek, it seemed to define a new connection between them.

Quinn was aware of the weight that rested on the dowager countess. He could tell the depth of the love she felt for her granddaughter and knew how desperate she was for him to agree to her plan. And what reason could he give her for refusing?

Everything she offered him would only benefit him and the two little girls he'd been given responsibility for. Because of the money she offered him, he would be able to pay all of Robert's creditors, and be completely out of debt. He would be able to make improvements not only to the estate, but also to Willow-brook. And, of the utmost importance, he could continue with his work for the government. If something unforeseen happened, he would have a wife to look after his nieces.

The longer he considered what the dowager countess offered him, the more he realized he had a huge decision to make.

Before he could speak, she placed her wine glass on the table next to her.

"And, I suppose you'd like to meet the woman I expect you to take as your wife before you agree to marry her."

"As you wish, my lady. But please be warned. If your grand-daughter objects to your plan, I will refuse your offer. I will not take a hostile bride, or one whose intent is to make my life a living hell."

"Nor would I expect you to, my lord. Now," Lady Granville turned and rang a bell that sat on the table beside her. Before the echo of the bell stopped ringing, the butler opened the door and stepped inside the room.

"Yes, my lady."

"Would you see if my granddaughter is awake, Converse?"

"Yes, my lady." The butler left, then returned within minutes. "Lady Cassandra is awake and prepared to receive visitors."

"Good. Lord Rosemont and I will go up."

"Yes, my lady."

Converse left the room and Lady Granville held out her hand for Quinn to take.

"I believe it is time for you to meet your future wife, my lord."

He scowled. "My lady, I—"

She simply patted his hand. "Yes, yes. We'll deal with all that in due time."

Quinn helped Lady Granville to her feet, then assisted her up the stairs. His heart raced with each step he took, and the blood roared in his ears. He felt the same as he always did right before a battle, hoping he'd survive, and fearing that he would not.

Chapter Four

CASSIE TURNED HER head when a knock sounded at the door. She was certain it was her grandmother's gentle rap. She came several times a day and Cassie always looked forward to her visits. At least she would carry on a conversation that was interesting enough that Cassie could ignore the pain that still ravaged her body.

From the moment she'd been struck by the horse, all she'd done was sleep. Today she'd risen from the bed and after a slow and painful process, managed to get dressed. It felt good, almost as though she might survive the whole ordeal. She'd even walked the length of the hall earlier, evidence that she was definitely improving.

She would love to blame the man who'd struck her for her injuries, but that wouldn't be fair. It wasn't his fault. It was hers.

She was the one who'd darted out into the street without looking. She'd had her head down to avoid the pelting rain. If only she'd been watching, she could have escaped the pain that wracked her body. It was a fact that she would have had a better chance of stopping than a rider on a horse might.

Cassie focused on her grandmother as she entered the room. Her gait wasn't as steady as it had been just weeks earlier, nor did she seem as spry. Cassie reminded herself to ask her grandmother if she was feeling well. She seemed more pale than usual.

"Good morning, Grandmama."

"Good morning, sweetling. How are you feeling?"

"Better. Much better."

Cassie reached out and hugged her grandmother. Only then did she see the tall, broad-shouldered man standing in the doorway.

He was a stranger to her, yet Cassie felt as though she'd met him before. The man had shoulders broad enough to take up most of the doorway. His hair was a dark brown, the color of mahogany, and it was a little longer than most men wore their hair. His complexion was a light bronze, as if he spent a great deal of his time out of doors. Cassie was forced to lift her gaze to meet his eyes, he was that tall.

"Cassie, I'd like you to meet Lord Quinten Beckham, Earl of Rosemont."

"You're the man who saved me when I ran in front of your horse. Thank you."

"The honor was mine, Lady Cassandra. Although I believe I played a major part in causing the mishap."

Cassie couldn't help but smile. It was obvious the man had placed the blame on his shoulders. She wanted to argue with him, but knew it would do no good.

"Be that as it may, I still thank you for rescuing me. I wouldn't have blamed you if you'd have left me in the street. I know I frightened your horse terribly. You're an excellent horseman if you stayed atop your mount in such inclement weather."

"I've had a great deal of experience riding."

"Lord Rosemont was a Colonel in the war, Cassie," her grandmother said.

"Oh," Cassie answered. "Was it as horrible as I've heard?"

"I'm not sure what you heard, but I'd venture to say it was worse."

Cassie studied the vacant look in Lord Rosemont's eyes. "You don't like to talk about your time in Crimea, do you?"

"It's not a time in my life I wish to remember. Or relive."

"Then we will talk of more pleasant topics. Please, be seated."

Cassie noticed her grandmother was already seated. The stranger moved a chair near to where her grandmother sat.

"Did you come to see if I had any lasting effects from my accident?" Cassie asked.

Lord Rosemont smiled. "I found I couldn't put the event out of my mind until I discovered how you fared."

"How considerate of you, but I am making great strides at recovering every day. I've even tried every form of enticement to convince Grandmama that I am well enough to take a walk in the garden."

"But she's refused?"

"Yes. She doesn't want me to overdo it. But frankly, my lord, being confined to these four walls has tested my sanity."

"Perhaps Lord Rosemont would agree to accompany you on a short walk in the garden," her grandmother said in a questioning voice. "I feel confident he would make sure you didn't stay out too long."

"It would be my pleasure."

"I'm not sure…" she started to say, but her grandmother reached over and placed her hand over Cassie's.

"It will be all right, Cassie. I'm sure Lord Rosemont won't allow you to overdo your first time out-of-doors."

Cassie focused her gaze on the earl's supportive expression. She took a huge breath in an effort to calm her insides. "Yes, I'm sure he will." She turned her head to look at her grandmother. "Would you like to accompany us?"

"No, dear. I think I would like to rest for a while. I'm suddenly quite tired."

Her grandmother rose with them and led the way out of Cassie's bedroom, but turned toward her own room when Cassie and the earl walked down the hall in the opposite direction.

The Earl of Rosemont extended his arm for her to take, and she placed her fingers on his coat sleeve. In her weakened state, she clasped his arm more firmly for support and was startled when her body reacted keenly to the feel of his muscled arm. Her abdomen tightened and the beating of her heart thundered erratically in her breast.

Her reaction was totally unexpected. She wasn't used to feeling any physical emotion when on the arm of a stranger. Neither did she exhibit a reaction when in a man's arms on the dance floor. Why she responded to the Earl of Rosemont's nearness was a mystery to her now.

Together, they walked down the stairs. When they reached the ground floor, he led her across the foyer, then into the library and out the double French doors that took them across the terrace. He was so very gentle as he assisted her down the three cement steps that led into the garden, and though she was already tired, she allowed him to lead her along the central path.

"Are you all right, Lady Cassandra?"

Cassie looked around the garden, then took in the cloudless sky. The sun shone amazingly bright and cast rays that kept her warm.

"Yes, my lord. I am perfectly fine. I didn't realize how much I missed being out-of-doors."

Cassie matched the smile he blessed her with and took note of how startlingly handsome Lord Rosemont was. And how different he was from any other man of her acquaintance. No brash ego, no cloying compliments—just pure manly attentiveness.

"Perhaps we should sit for a moment," the colonel suggested when they reached a wrought-iron bench beneath a spreading shade tree.

"Yes. Please. I'm afraid my strength is not fully returned."

He led her to the bench and she released a pent-up sigh as she sat.

"Do you need to return to the house?"

"Oh, no!" Cassie answered. "I love the outdoors. I've waited for what seems like forever to be able to return to the garden. It's far too soon to go back inside."

Cassie lifted her chin and let the sun breaking through the shade warm her face. There was a gentle breeze that made her feel alive when it brushed over her. She couldn't help but smile when her face warmed, and the breeze blew her hair from her face. She opened her eyes and found the colonel looking at her.

"Please, excuse me," she said softly, lowering her gaze in embarrassment. "It is just that it has been so long since I've enjoyed being in the out-of-doors."

"I'm pleased that I could play a part in your enjoyment, my lady. Seeing your reaction to the day made me appreciate the sunshine and fresh air all the more."

Cassie felt her cheeks warm with embarrassment. Even though she didn't expect to, she realized she felt very comfortable with Lord Rosemont. "Allow me to express my sympathy on the passing of your brother and sister-in-law," she said when she lifted her gaze to his. "To suffer two such losses so close to each other must have been terribly difficult."

"Yes," the colonel answered. "It was. I didn't expect to lose Robert so soon. Nor did I ever think I would be forced to assume the Rosemont title."

Cassie was surprised at what the colonel revealed. "I'm sure that was a sad but welcome happenstance."

He smiled. "Actually, it was not. I was never envious of Robert's position in the family. I far more enjoyed doing the physical work on our estate than being tied down behind a desk."

"My father was a great deal like that, too," Cassie said. "Which was why he taught me to take care of the books while he oversaw the land."

"You took care of your father's books?"

"I did. He would much rather be out in the open than sequestered within four walls of a study."

"He sounds like someone I would have got along with quite well."

Cassie lifted her head until her gaze locked with his. "I think you would have been quite amicable, indeed." She smiled. "He also enjoyed living in the country much better than the city.

Lord Rosemont smiled. "If I had my choice, I would reside in the country and never venture to the city but once or twice a year."

"Don't you think that will be possible for you now?"

"Perhaps it will be at present, but the time will come when I'll have to spend more time in London. I am responsible for Robert and Elaine's two daughters. The time will come when I will have to arrange the girls' come-outs."

"Oh, yes. I heard your brother left you with two nieces. What are their ages?"

"Molly is five months and Lizzy is five years."

"Oh, they're but babies, still."

"Yes. I wasn't prepared to be an instant father, let alone both mother and father, but life often presents one with challenges."

"Yes, life does."

Cassie tried to hide the fact that she not only agreed with him about those challenges, but she knew from experience exactly what he meant. It seemed like yesterday when her world fell apart like his must have seemed to shatter when his brother and his sister-in-law died and left their children in his care. Only she did not lose a brother or a sister. She lost the man to whom she'd given her heart.

Cassie thought back to the day of her wedding. It was a beautiful spring day. So many sprigs of lilacs decorated the church that it was impossible to find an empty space for more. The pews were lined with bouquets of lilacs and in the front of the church, where she and the man she would marry would stand, an archway was stuffed with the fragrant purple blossoms.

Cassie took in a deep breath, and as if it were only yesterday and she was back in the church, the fragrant smell of lilacs filled her nose. She closed her eyes and the man who was to be her husband appeared before her.

He was tall, handsome, with blond hair and blue eyes as deep as a cloudless blue sky on a clear summer's day. He was the man Cassie thought she loved. The man she thought loved her. But he didn't.

She remembered waiting for Evan to show up for their wedding. She relived the agonizing embarrassment when hour after hour passed, and he failed to appear.

Her grandmother left the church, and came to be with her. There were no words to make the humiliation Cassie felt go away. Her grandmother did the only thing she knew to do. She nestled Cassie's ice cold hands in her own and tried to comfort her while they waited in vain for the love of her life to appear. But he didn't.

Eventually, Cassie's uncle spoke to the congregation, explaining that everyone could go home, that there wouldn't be a wedding.

When the church was empty, her grandmother rose and encouraged Cassie to go home. But Cassie refused to go. To leave would be an admission that the man she thought she loved didn't love her. The man to whom she'd given her heart didn't want it.

Later, she found out that Evan Walters, the gentleman she thought would be her husband, had eloped with one of Cassie's closest friends.

Cassie would never forget that day. She would never inhale the fragrant smell of lilacs in the spring without reliving that mortifying day. And from that day on, Cassie vowed that she would never endure such shame and humiliation again. She would never trust her heart to another man only to have it broken. She would never marry again.

She came out of her reverie and turned her attention back to the man sitting beside her.

"Who looks after your nieces when you are absent?" she asked, focusing her gaze on the faraway look in his eyes. Everything about him intrigued her. There was so much more she wanted to know about him. It was obvious that he'd been hurt as deeply as she had.

"Actually, there are several capable women who take care of them. There is Chloe Portsmouth. She's a relative of our vicar and she lives in, and takes care of them most of the time. Then there is Mrs. Rightworth. She can only care for them part-time, but she is the most wonderful nursemaid I could have hoped to find for them. They adore her."

"I'm glad you found two women so perfect. It's difficult to grow up without a mother."

"You sound as if you are speaking from experience."

"I am. My mother died when I was ten, but my father did his best to take her place. Plus, I had my grandmother. She was an ideal replacement for my mother. I couldn't have asked for anyone more perfect."

They sat in companionable silence a little while longer before Cassie felt the need to continue their walk. "I'd like to check on the roses, if you don't mind."

"Of course not," he said, with a smile that sent waves of warmth rushing through her.

The colonel rose and held out his hand for Cassie to take. There was nothing earth-shattering in the currents that shot through her, yet the feel of her hand in his caused a warmth she wasn't expecting.

They walked past the center tree, stopping once or twice to admire the roses, then turned to circle a small pond that was shaded by the center tree.

"Do you have a garden at Rosemont Manor?"

"Yes, we do. I try to take the girls out every day, weather permitting. Lizzy enjoys skipping down the garden walks. I got her a puppy, and it follows her wherever she goes."

"Oh, what kind of puppy?"

The colonel looked at her and shrugged his shoulders. "I'm not really sure. It's small. Rievers, my valet cum butler, tells me it's like the dog our Queen favors."

"Oh! A King Charles spaniel. They're wonderful dogs. What has she named it?"

"She calls it Puppy, although I tell her it won't stay a puppy for long."

"Oh, how darling."

"I take it you are fond of dogs."

"Oh, yes."

"Do you have one?"

"No. Unfortunately, Grandmother sneezes constantly when she's around dogs."

"And do you?"

"Sneeze?" Cassie laughed. "No. I'm quite content around animals. We had three dogs when my father was still alive. I grew up around pets."

"How old were you when you lost your father?"

"He died suddenly when I was eighteen. That's when I came to live with my grandmother."

They walked a little further, then the colonel slowed and looked down at her. "I think you are getting tired," he said, turning around to go back.

"Perhaps a little. But I so enjoyed our walk."

"I could tell you did. As I enjoyed being here with you."

The colonel hooked her arm through his and led her back to the house. When they reached the terrace, he walked with her through the library, then to the foyer.

"I truly enjoyed our conversation, my lady," he said, then lifted her hand to his lips and kissed her fingers.

"So did I," she said, then stood near the entrance when the butler opened the door.

Cassie watched him leave, then returned to the library. She needed time to herself. She had many emotions rushing through her that she needed to sort out. Emotions she hadn't felt for a very long time. Emotions she thought she'd never feel again.

CASSIE SAT IN one of the comfortable over-sized, cushioned chairs in the library and tried to read. But how could she concentrate on the words in her book when her mind refused to think of anything except the afternoon she'd spent with the Earl of Rosemont?

No matter how often she relived it, she couldn't explain her reaction to the earl. It was almost as if he was a long-time friend. Someone she'd known—and trusted—her entire life. But he wasn't. She'd just met him. She should have been wary of him, the same as she was distrustful of every other man with whom she came into contact.

Cassie closed the book in frustration and placed it on the table beside her chair. She'd never been so confused. No matter how hard she struggled to find answers, there weren't any to be found.

In frustration, she started to rise from her chair, but stopped when her grandmother entered the room.

"Am I interrupting you?"

"Of course not, Grandmama. Come, sit with me."

Converse brought her over to a chair next to Cassie and helped her grandmother sit.

"Have Cook send in some tea, Converse."

"Right away, my lady."

"What were you reading, Cassie?"

Cassie looked over to the book she'd placed on the table and had to read the title. "Obviously nothing that held my attention," Cassie laughed. "I can't even remember the title of the book."

Her grandmother chuckled. "That means you had something else on your mind that was more important."

"I suppose perhaps I did," Cassie answered. She paused when Converse brought in their tea tray, then Cassie poured the tea and handed her grandmother a cup.

"Close the door behind you, Converse."

"Yes, my lady."

Cassie looked at her grandmother and saw the lack of color in her face and the weariness in her eyes. "Is something wrong,

Grandmama?"

"No, Cassandra. I just tire easily these days."

Cassie felt a twinge of concern.

"I need to discuss something with you, my sweet. Something I'm afraid you're going to find very difficult."

Cassie's heart shifted in her breast. "What is it?"

"Have you thought what's going to happen to you when I'm no longer here?"

Cassie didn't want to have this conversation. She knew her grandmother was getting older, and she'd known without having to be told that her grandmother wasn't well. But, she didn't want to think of her no longer being with her.

"Don't think that way, Grandmama. You're going to be here for a long time yet."

"No, I'm not, Cassie. And you know it." Her grandmother paused. "I don't intend to die today or tomorrow, but I can't live forever, you know."

"Perhaps not forever, Grandmama. But years and years yet."

Cassie felt tears well in her eyes and knew she wouldn't be able to keep them from spilling down her cheeks. She didn't want to think of her grandmother dying. She didn't want to think of being alone for the rest of her life.

Her grandmother smiled. "No, Cassie. Not even one or two."

Cassie fell to her knees in front of her grandmother and clasped her hands. Her grandmother had been both mother and father to her since the day her father had died.

"Cassie," her grandmother whispered, then ran one thin, frail finger down Cassie's cheek. "We have to decide what will happen to you when I'm no longer here."

Cassie tried to shut out her grandmother's words, but they came through even when Cassie didn't want to hear them.

"I won't ever be alone. There's father's younger brothers, Gerald, the Earl of Granville, and Uncle William."

"But you can't count on them to help you should you ever need anything," her grandmother interrupted. "Either of them.

Especially your uncle Gerald. I'm afraid he knows the massive amount your father left you and will do everything in his power to gain control of your money the moment I am not here to stop him."

"What are you saying, Grandmother?"

"I'm saying you cannot rely on either of your uncles for your livelihood. You cannot be dependent on them for even a roof over your head."

Tears fell freely from Cassie's eyes. Her grandmother was forcing her to face her worst fears. "Oh, Grandmama," she cried, "It can't be so!"

"Stand, Cassandra. We will face our futures without cowering. You've faced worse tragedies in your short life. You will face this, too. And survive."

After she stood, Cassie walked to the fireplace and stared at the lifeless logs in the grate. She clutched her hands at her sides. "What is it you are suggesting I do, Grandmama?"

"Marry, Cassie."

Cassie spun to face her. "No, Grandmama! You know I will not trust my heart to another man!"

"What I know is that you don't have a choice. Not if you don't want to rely on one of your uncles to provide you with a home. Or worse yet, you find it necessary to travel from one relative to the next when you wear out your welcome. Or have to beg for the little pocket money you will ever have. Or, always feel as if you are the spare that someone in your family feels obligated to accompany to any social event or concert or theater performance you wish to attend."

Cassie couldn't stop the tears from spilling from her eyes. "Why are you making things seem so bleak? Why are you presenting everything as being so hopeless?"

"Because I want you to face your future as it will be if you don't make a life for yourself. I love you, Cassie, but there is so much more to life than being dependent on your family for what you have. You need a home of your own and a family of your own."

"Which I will never have," Cassie wailed, "and you know why, Grandmama. Those dreams were taken away from me a long time ago."

"But there is a way for you to get them back."

Cassie froze where she stood. She swiped the tears from her eyes and stared at her grandmother. What was she saying? She knew she could never trust a man enough to marry him.

"No, Grandmama. It's too late. I'm too broken to be a wife to any man."

"What if I told you there was someone who has promised to take you as his wife? Who has promised to care for you and provide for you? And provide you children if you want them."

Cassie stared at her grandmother in disbelief. "Who?"

"The Earl of Rosemont."

Cassie stumbled back a few steps and sank into the cushioned chair beside her grandmother. "Who?"

"The Earl of Rosemont, dear."

"Why…? What…? How do you know…?"

Cassie sat in silence for several long seconds as she considered what her grandmother was telling her.

"Listen to me, Cassie. Think over what I'm about to suggest and don't close your mind to what I propose until you've considered the alternatives."

Cassie clasped her hands in her lap and prepared to listen. She was certain she would feel the same when her grandmother finished as she did now, but at least Grandmama would think she'd given her suggestion due consideration.

"Very well," Cassie finally said.

"When your cousin Ira heard that you had nearly been run down by the Earl of Rosemont, he came to call. He related to me that the Earl of Rosemont came home from the war to find that he had assumed the Rosemont title. He also discovered that his brother had not only left him in dire financial straits, but that he'd also become guardian of his brother's two children, one just a babe."

"Yes, he told me as much."

"I offered to pay his debts in exchange for your hand in marriage."

"Grandmother! No!"

"Yes, Cassie."

"How could you? You know I have settled my mind to never marry. And you know why!"

"I don't know his reasons, but Lord Rosemont feels the same."

Cassie sat in stunned silence for several moments, then offered her grandmother the first argument she thought of. "If you offered Lord Rosemont a large enough amount of money that he would be able to pay all of his debts, why won't you give that amount to me so I can purchase a small manor house in which to live, as well as to have an adequate allowance to live on my own?"

"Because you would not be on your own. The moment word circulated that you had come into a large amount of money in trust, not only would you be hounded by every money-seeking rogue who is desperate to lay claim to your wealth, but your biggest adversaries would be your uncles. They would both hound you for the wealth you inherited. And they would not stop until one of them had control of it. You would not have a peaceful day from that time on."

Cassie wanted to argue with her grandmother, but she couldn't. Her grandmother was correct. She could see the parade of men vying for her hand in order to force her into marriage. And, she could see her uncles doing everything in their power to take every last shilling away from her.

"What did Lord Rosemont say when you proposed a marriage between us?"

"He refused at first, the same as you. But after some thought, I believe he realized that for the sake of the two babes for whom he is responsible, he doesn't have a choice. He asked me for time to think things over and consider my offer."

Cassie sat in shock.

"I also made him promise to give you however much time you wanted or needed to agree to be his wife in the true sense of the word."

"He agreed to enter into a marriage in name only?" Cassie asked in disbelief.

"Yes, he did."

"Did he say why?"

"No, and I didn't press him on the matter."

"Did he state any other stipulations to your offer?"

"Only one."

Cassie felt a certain amount of curiosity. "What was that?"

"That the decision of whether to marry would be yours alone, and that you not be *forced* to marry, but enter the agreement willingly. He was adamant that you not feel as though you are being forced to do something you do not wish to do."

Cassie thought about what her grandmother said for several moments. The decision was hers to make and she could accept or refuse at her will.

"May I have time to think about this?"

"Of course, Cassie. I don't plan on dying before morning. I intend to see you happily settled before I leave you."

"Oh, Grandmama." Cassie struggled to halt the tears forming in her eyes.

"Don't weep for me, sweetling. I'm actually looking forward to that new part of my life. I've missed your grandfather terribly since he died, and I look forward to being with him again. Always remember how happy I'll be."

Cassie rose and wrapped her arms around her grandmother. She didn't know how she would get along without the dear woman, but death was part of life, and Cassie would learn to survive that part...just as she'd survived when her parents had both died and the man she was convinced she loved with all her heart left her for someone else.

Only one aspect of her grandmother's proposal gave Cassie any consolation. She alone would determine what she would do with her life. She alone would decide *if*—and *who*—she married.

The choice was solely hers to make.

CHAPTER FIVE

C ASSIE SAT IN the drawing room and waited for the Earl of
Rosemont to arrive. Yesterday she'd sent a message
requesting that he meet with her to discuss the possibility of
marrying without consummating their marriage until they at
least knew each other better. She couldn't imagine making love
to a stranger. But neither could she imagine marrying a stranger.

Then again, she'd promised herself to a man she thought she
knew as well as she knew herself and been betrayed by him.

What made her think she could trust the Earl of Rosemont—
a man she didn't know at all—to give her his word and keep it?

But according to her grandmother, the earl wasn't at all like
the Marquess of Weatherly. He would never elope with her best
friend and leave her stranded at the altar. And Lord Rosemont
seemed agreeable to her demand that they get to know each
other better before they chose to consummate their marriage.
Still, Cassie needed to hear that promise for herself.

Cassie heard voices in the foyer and knew he was here. She
rose and waited for him to join her, working hard to still a
nervous tremor.

"Lord Rosemont, my lady," Converse announced from the
doorway.

"Thank you, Converse."

Cassie stared at the man with whom she would possibly share

the rest of her life and her heart shifted in her breast. He was so appealing, so handsome and poised, that anyone would surely wonder at her good fortune. She wasn't usually moved by the angle of a chiseled jaw, or deep russet eyes one could drown in, but it seemed today would be an exception.

She knew she had never been considered a beauty, but when placed next to the man facing her, she was more aware than ever how plain and ordinary she appeared.

Although she'd never thought of herself as delicate or petite, compared to the giant of a man whose broad shoulders and towering height seemed to fill the doorway, she suddenly felt very diminutive in comparison.

"Please, Lord Rosemont. Come in."

"Good day, Lady Cassandra," he said, then walked to her. He took her hand and brought her fingers to his lips.

"Please, have a chair."

He did. He sat across from her so they could look each other in the eye. Cassie thought she should feel intimidated by his nearness, but she didn't. She felt surprisingly comfortable with him. She was aware of how improper it was for her to be alone with a male caller, but this occasion was hardly ordinary.

"I take it the dowager countess spoke to you about her proposal."

Cassie felt her cheeks grow warm. "Yes, my lord. She also said you asked for time to consider her offer."

"I did. Before I give your grandmother an answer, I want to talk to you privately. I want to ask you a question."

"Yes?"

He looked at her with a serious expression. "Please, consider your answer carefully. Your future depends upon your decision."

Cassie couldn't stop a smile from forming. "Are you trying to frighten me from accepting your proposition?"

"If that is how you'd like to consider it. The choice is yours. Completely yours."

The expression on the Earl of Rosemont's face turned even

more serious—the words from his rich, rumbling voice as tender as she'd ever heard. The tone of his voice as calming as Cassie could imagine.

"You have this chance to refuse what your grandmother wants for you. I would never force you to enter into this arrangement if you are not in complete agreement with it."

"And if I refuse?" Cassie asked. She kept her eyes locked with his, hoping to see an indication of his feelings. "What will happen to you?"

A smile lifted the corners of his mouth, changing his rugged features into looks more handsome than any man had a right to possess. "Do not worry about me, my lady. I've survived this long and will, God willing, survive longer still. What is important is that you do not regret the decision you make today."

"And the children, your lordship? How will they fare if you refuse?"

She watched him react ever so slightly to her question with well-masked embarrassment. He averted his eyes.

Cassie rose. On legs that trembled beneath her, she walked to the double French doors and stared beyond the terrace to the garden below.

"Before I give you my answer, I would like to hear exactly what you expect of me. Every detail," she said softly.

The earl paused several moments before answering.

"All right then. As you know, I am deeply in debt. Your grandmother offered to award me a substantial amount of money to pay my brother's creditors in exchange for your hand in marriage."

Cassie turned her head to look at the man she would take as her husband. "And what am I to do in exchange for the money my grandmother has promised you?"

"I would ask that you be mistress of Rosemont Manor. I give you free rein to run our home as you see fit, oversee the staff, and make any changes or improvements you wish to make."

"That is all?"

The Earl of Rosemont paused, and Cassie turned. His expression indicated that there was another matter he wanted to address, but was reluctant to ask. The knot that formed in the pit of her stomach told her that the matter he didn't want to bring up was something he feared she would regret knowing.

Cassie took a deep breath and prepared to refuse to marry him even though there were several advantages to their union.

"Yes, my lord? Is there something more?"

"Two matters, Lady Cassandra. But before I say what they are, I want you to know that only one of them is contingent upon our marriage agreement."

Cassie stepped closer to the earl. She sat in the chair beside his. He followed suit and sat in the chair next to her.

"I would like to hear the matter that is not contingent upon our marriage agreement first, if you would be so kind."

"Yes, of course. As you know, my brother and his wife left behind two small children. Two little girls, one of five years, the other only five months."

"Yes, you spoke of them when we last met."

"Yes, well, I would ask you to secure an appropriate staff to look after them. To entertain them occasionally. To teach them women's ways and see to their education. And, um, and if you can find it in your heart to check on them every once in a while, I would greatly appreciate it. I would like them to feel wanted and accepted by you, and know what it is to have a woman's attention and influence."

The breath caught in Cassie's throat. Did he think she would object to being mother to two babes who'd lost their parents? Her heart ached that he thought she might be so cold.

"I don't expect you to be a mother to children who are not your own, but I would appreciate it if you could show them a small amount of compassion."

"Then that point is of no consequence, my lord," Cassie said in all seriousness. "I would be honored to be part of your nieces' lives. No child should grow up without a mother's love. If we marry, you may be assured that I will do my best to care for your nieces as if they were my own."

The Earl of Rosemont closed his eyes as if relieved by her answer, then opened them and looked at her. "Thank you, my lady. I can't tell you how appreciative I am that you feel as you do."

"And the second point? The point that is contingent upon our marrying?"

"It is my work, my lady."

Cassie couldn't hide her surprise. "Your work?"

"Yes. I have certain…obligations to Her Majesty. Obligations I refuse to abandon."

Cassie sat in silence for several moments. "Are these…obligations…dangerous?"

A slight smile lifted the corners of his mouth. "I do not consider them dangerous. Simply important."

"And they take you away from Rosemont Estate on occasion?"

"Yes, my lady. Sometimes for several days, even weeks, at a time."

"I see," she said. "And you refuse to give up your work even after we marry?"

"Yes, my lady."

Cassie considered what Lord Rosemont was saying. If she read him correctly, the work he did for the government would always be more important than her or their marriage.

Well, at least he was open about that before they married.

"Very well. I can agree to that. Is there anything else?"

"No, my lady. Other than to assure you that you will always have an adequate amount of money at your disposal, to spend any way you like. Anything you need, you only have to purchase, and send me the bill. You will also have an account of your own to make purchases above and beyond household expenditures."

Cassie nodded at his generosity. She'd never been overindulgent, and didn't intend to be so now, but she didn't want to live in a house that was falling down around her ears, or in one where the coverings on the furniture were worn through. Or the carpets on the floors were threadbare.

"That's very kind of you, my lord."

The Earl of Rosemont hesitated before he spoke. Cassie could see by the deep furrows on his forehead that he was considering how to bring up the topic of intimacy between them and didn't know how to broach the subject. Cassie decided she needed to be the one to introduce such a delicate subject. She was, after all, the one who'd issued the demand that he give her time before expecting her to consent to intimacy between them.

"I believe the only aspect of our marriage we haven't discussed is the personal side of our union. My grandmother said she told you about my stipulation."

"Yes, she did."

"She also told me that you didn't have any objections to that stipulation. But I would like to hear your agreement with my own ears. Do you promise that you will give us adequate time to get to know one another before you demand your husbandly rights?"

"Yes. I do."

Cassie rose from her chair and walked to the lifeless fireplace. "Thank you, Lord Rosemont."

The earl didn't move for several moments, then walked to a side table where decanters were kept and poured a glass of wine and a glass of brandy. He handed Cassie the wine and he kept the brandy.

"I think we should drink to our agreement," he said lifting his glass. "I want you to know that I am not a man of violence, and am not so set in my ways that I will find it impossible to change. You only have to inform me of anything you would like me to alter."

Cassie lifted her glass. "I am not prone to anger or to shrill complaining. I will gladly alter any habits you discover about me that you do not like. I am mostly fond of reading, and of working in the garden."

"And I am mostly fond of riding my land, and reading." He looked up at her. "Do you ride?"

"Yes, my lord. I am quite fond of riding."

He smiled. "Good. I will get you a horse as soon as we're settled."

"I would like that," Cassie said.

"To our new adventure," he said, bringing his glass to his mouth.

"To our new adventure," Cassie repeated, then took a swallow of her wine.

"Is there anything else you'd like to discuss?" Cassie asked when she lowered her glass.

"One thing," he answered. "My name is Quinten. But I would appreciate it if you called me Quinn."

"Quinn," Cassie said and was pleased that the name rolled off her tongue in a natural way. "And my name is Cassandra, but everyone calls me Cassie."

"Cassie," he repeated. "The name suits you."

"All that remains," Cassie said, "is to make plans for our marriage."

"Do you prefer a large wedding, or a more private affair?"

"If you have no preference, my lord, I would prefer a small, private affair."

"I don't mind at all, my lady. I will get a special license as soon as possible, and I'll let you and your grandmother make all the arrangements. Perhaps we can even have the wedding here if that pleases you."

"Yes," Cassie said.

The Earl of Rosemont placed his glass on the table, then turned his head to face her. "I feel as if I should seal our agreement with a kiss." And he lowered his head and did just that.

His kiss wasn't filled with passion or lust, or anything close to those emotions. Yet it was the most tender and intimate kiss she'd ever received. He broke it off far too soon for her liking, but she was glad. Any longer and she was afraid she would have burst into flames.

"Just know that I appreciate what you and your grandmother have done for me," he said taking her hands in his.

Cassie smiled. "Perhaps you'd like to come again tomorrow or the next day to finalize everything with Grandmother."

"Yes. I'd like that."

The Earl of Rosemont bowed politely, then left the room.

When he was gone, Cassie sat down on the sofa and clutched her hands in her lap. She was going to be married. She was going to have what she'd dreamed of having until the day all her dreams had been destroyed.

There was even the possibility that she might have children of her own. She'd always dreamed of having a large family. Cassie had grown up alone and had missed having brothers and sisters to play with, and talk to, and confide in. A marriage to Lord Rosemont might be the opportunity to have the children she'd always longed for.

And even if she didn't have children of her own, she would have the earl's two nieces to look after. They could be her children.

Cassie thought of the man with whom she would spend her future and sighed in contentment. She found him easy to talk to, and easy to be around. Unless he was not the man he pretended to be, she could envision a happy future.

CHAPTER SIX

QUINN SPENT THE morning obtaining the special license, then returned to see the Dowager Countess of Granville. He signed the necessary papers and came away with enough money to pay his creditors plus enough in the bank to begin several improvements to Rosemont Estate that he'd only dreamed of being able to make.

When all the arrangements were made, he and Lady Casandra were married in a small service in the Dowager Countess of Granville's London town house.

Cassie's grandmother was present, along with the dowager countess's two sons and one daughter. It was obvious they were surprised to receive word that their niece was marrying, since they considered her well on the shelf and they'd heard no rumors of her being courted by anyone. It was also obvious that they silently questioned Quinn's motives for marrying their niece, and resented Quinn for ruining their plans to gain great wealth. But they didn't ask his reasons or comment on them, although Quinn knew that before the day was over, they would confront him. Quinn looked forward to their conversation. It was important that they clear the air before he and Cassie left for Rosemont.

Theo was there, along with Jack. Quinn couldn't conceive of marrying without his two closest friends at his side. Besides, he needed them to bring a wagon for anything Cassie wanted to transport to her new home, as well as a carriage for her and her lady's maid. He wanted the journey to be as comfortable as possible.

When the ceremony was over and he and Cassie had signed the marriage license, they all enjoyed the wedding breakfast. Quinn watched his new bride and noticed how many times she glanced at her grandmother. It was as if she were memorizing every detail of her facial features, in case this was the last time she saw her. Quinn experienced a pang of concern for his new wife. He knew how difficult this was for her. Without thinking, he reached over and placed his hand atop her hands that lay clenched in her lap.

The second his hands touched hers, she stiffened with a start.

"I'm sorry, my lady," he whispered. "I didn't mean to startle you. I just want you to know that I realize how difficult this is for you."

"You just surprised me," she said, then smiled. "I will become accustomed to such familiarities in time."

Quinn gave her fingers a gentle squeeze, then lifted his hand away.

The wedding guests finished their food while stopping at intervals to issue a toast to the bride and groom. Before the meal was over, the dowager countess's oldest son issued a final toast. He welcomed Quinn into the family and wished the newlyweds a long and happy life. But it was obvious he didn't mean his words. The hostile glare in his eyes made it clear that he resented Quinn for taking away the money that went with Cassie.

There were one or two more toasts before the breakfast came to a conclusion, but thankfully, no one expected the bride and groom to show any sign of familiarity. There was no raucous suggestion that the groom kiss the bride or display any sign of affection. It was as if they all knew the bride and groom were not well acquainted, yet no one said a word.

When the breakfast concluded, the guests rose and moved to a large salon. Quinn and Cassie stood, but Cassie didn't move with the rest of the guests.

"Would you mind if I stayed behind with my grandmother for a moment? I'd like to tell her goodbye in private."

"Of course. Are your belongings packed?"

"Yes. They're sitting at the top of the stairs. Converse will show you."

"Take your time, Cassie. We won't leave until you're ready."

She smiled and Quinn had the strongest urge to squeeze her hand just a little to show her that he understood how difficult this moment was and indicate that he sympathized with her. But he remembered her reaction the last time he touched her and kept his hands at his sides.

He watched her walk away from him and went to find Jack and Theo to get Cassie's trunks and load them in the wagon. They'd have to be on their way as soon as she finished saying goodbye to her grandmother. The longer she stayed, the harder it would be for her to leave.

CASSIE WALKED TO where her grandmother sat at the end of the table and wrapped her arms around the woman who'd been a mother to her for nearly half her life. She knew she wouldn't have survived if not for the love and guidance her grandmother had given her from the day Cassie's mother had died. She knew she would not be as strong as she was today if not for the strength her grandmother had instilled in her.

And yet, knowing this might be the last time she saw her grandmother made her feel as if she weren't strong at all. She'd never felt more adrift.

"I'm not sure I can do this, Grandmama," Cassie whispered as she hugged her grandmother.

"You can, sweetling. You must. You have found a perfect man to look after you and care for you."

Cassie smiled through her tears. "You found him, Grandmama. You recognized his goodness and arranged for me to have a life separate from the threats and greed of anyone who only wanted me for my money."

"No. I was not the one who ran in front of his horse. You were."

Cassie forced a small laugh. "I guess you're right." Cassie clutched her grandmother's hands and held on tight. "I'm going to make him a horrible wife. You know that. And I'm afraid he's going to regret ever laying eyes on me."

"No. Every day he thinks of what you brought to your marriage he'll be thankful he met you."

"What made you so sure he would be someone I would be happy with?"

Her grandmother lifted her hand and cupped Cassie's cheek. Her grandmother's eyes filled with a longing Cassie wasn't used to seeing in her grandmother's eyes. A faraway look that left Cassie feeling as if she was searching for something—or someone—she missed.

"Because he reminded me of my Matthew. There was a strength about him, a softness that indicated he was capable of great compassion. And when he returned to make sure you had survived, I knew there was something very special about him. He was a man you could get to know and love."

"I hope you're right, Grandmama. I would so like to learn to love the man I married. To care for him so deeply that I could not live without him."

"You will, my dear. I know you will. Just as I came to care for and love my Matthew."

The Dowager Countess of Granville lifted her gaze and watched her eldest son enter the room.

"There you are," the Earl of Granville said, coming closer.

"Did you need something, Gerald?" the dowager countess asked.

"No. I only wanted to bid my niece farewell and wish her all the best."

"Thank you, Uncle," Cassie said, seeing the deceitful glint in his eyes.

"I also wanted to make sure you knew that you always had a place in my home should you ever need to escape the disastrous marriage you've entered into."

Cassie took in a harsh breath. "What makes you think that my marriage will be a disaster? I believe I have found a perfectly wonderful man with whom to spend my life."

"What do you know about the man you married?"

"I know everything I need to know about him. At least he did not leave me standing at the altar on the day of our wedding."

"Perhaps that is because he desired your fortune too much to give it up."

"That's enough, Gerald." There was a formidable anger in the dowager countess's voice when she reprimanded her son. "Just because you have lost the fortune that went with Cassandra, doesn't mean you have the right to besmirch the man who will acquire it."

"And what, pray tell, do you know about the man your granddaughter has just married?"

"I know he is a good and admirable man. I know he has served honorably in Her Majesty's service and been awarded several medals by Her Majesty. And I know he does not have half as many vices as you and your brother have. If his father was still alive, he would be exceedingly proud of his son, whereas I know the same cannot be said of you, Lord Granville. Your father would not find one honorable bone in your miserable body. Nor that of your brother."

Her uncle's face lost its color at his mother's put-down.

"Thank you, Mother. I finally know exactly what your true feelings are for me."

"You have never hidden your faults and vices, Gerald. You left me no doubt as to your true nature. I am simply pointing out what you have proudly displayed for my knowledge."

"Well," the Earl of Granville said with haughty anger. "I wish you much happiness, Cassandra. I fear you will need it."

"And I am equally as certain that I will not, Uncle,"

With that retort, her uncle turned on his heel and left the room.

"Are you alright, Grandmama?" Cassie asked when they were alone.

"I am perfectly fine, Cassandra. In fact, I am better than fine. I have waited a long time for the opportunity to tell my son what I thought of his gaming and womanizing. I only wish his brother had been here to hear what I had to say."

"I don't doubt that you'll find the opportunity soon," Cassie said, kissing her grandmother on the cheek.

Cassie held her grandmother's hands and brought them to her lips and kissed them. When she placed them back in her grandmother's lap, her grandmother's gaze was focused on the open doorway. "Your prince awaits you, my darling."

Cassie followed her grandmother's gaze and saw Quinn standing beyond the open doorway. Her heart shifted enough to cause her breath to catch. She didn't know how it had happened, but the man she'd married stirred her greatly. She found she could spend hours every day just watching him.

"You'd best be going now, my sweet. Is Leann packed and ready to accompany you?"

"Yes, you know I couldn't go anywhere without her. Who would do my hair if not Leann? Thank you for allowing me to steal her away from you."

"You didn't steal her. She's been your lady's maid since you have lived with me."

Cassie looked at her grandmother and tears formed in her eyes.

"Don't be sad, my dear. Your future lies ahead of you. As does mine."

Cassie gave her grandmother another kiss goodbye, then swiped the tears from her eyes. "Goodbye, Grandmama. I love you."

Cassie gave her grandmother a final kiss on her withered cheek and walked to her husband.

She turned her head for a final farewell look, then left with a man she was terrified of being alone with, yet wasn't afraid of at all.

CASSIE AND LEANN rode in the Rosemont carriage as they made their way to her new home. Leann had fallen asleep shortly after they'd left London. She was the one who'd packed all Cassie's belongings as well as her own, so it was only understandable that she was tired.

Quinn rode his horse beside the carriage, while Jack Washburn sat atop the carriage and Theo Dunworthy rode on the other side of the carriage.

Quinn had explained that these men were fellow army officers he'd served with. But Cassie could tell they were more than fellow officers by the way they interacted with each other. They were friends of her husband's. Close friends.

Cassie looked out the window and watched how her husband handled his horse. He was an excellent horseman and exuded a power over the animal that was more than impressive. When he saw her watching him, he rode toward her.

"Would you mind if I rode inside for a while?" he asked when he reached their carriage.

"I would like that," she answered. "I have several questions I'd like to ask before we reach your home."

"*Our* home," he corrected, and Cassie smiled.

"Yes. Our home."

Her husband had their driver stop and he tied his horse to the back of the carriage, then stepped inside. He sat on the seat opposite her next to a sleeping Leann.

"How long will it be before we arrive?" she said when he was settled, and the carriage was moving again.

"A little over three hours. We're only five hours from London."

That wasn't so very far. She didn't know why she thought Rosemont Manor was farther from London than it was.

"Grandmother had Cook pack a lunch for us. Would you like to stop for a bit and have something to eat?"

He shook his head. "I prefer to keep moving. I want to get home before it turns dark. Besides," he said with a smile, "Jack and Theo are former army. They're used to going without regular meals. But I wouldn't refuse something to drink if Cook packed a bottle of something."

Cassie lifted the lid on the basket sitting beside her and brought out a flask. "Will brandy do?" she asked, handing him the silver flask.

"Perfectly," he said.

Quinn tilted the flask toward her with a raised eyebrow, clearly offering her a turn. She blushed and took back the flask to tuck it into the basket.

"Aha. Beautiful *and* an abstainer."

Cassie's blush deepened. "Not at all, sir!"

She certainly had no qualms about enjoying a good wine. But brandy? She made a rash decision and darted her hand back into the basket. Before she could think about it, she unscrewed the stopper and lifted the flask to her lips. Over the top of the flask she could see his eyes alive with delight as he watched her every movement.

Cassie opened her mouth and stopped. Just a moment ago his lips had caressed the mouth of the flask. What dangerous message might she send if she were to put her own lips upon it?

With surprising regret, Cassie put the brandy back into the basket and made a show of withdrawing the other bits of food Cook had packed.

Across from her Quinn chuckled.

"I intended to compliment you earlier," he said. "You made a beautiful bride. My men wasted no time telling me how lucky I was that you agreed to marry me."

Cassie felt her cheeks warm again. "I thank you for the compliment, although I'm not foolish enough to believe you. I am the fortunate one. You are far more handsome than I am attractive."

He stayed her hand as she was about to close the basket and retrieved the flask to take another swig of his brandy. "I can see I am going to have to strive to convince you of your beauty."

"I am not blind, my lord. I have looked in a mirror often enough to see the truth."

Cassie felt a warmth settle inside her.

"I suddenly realize that I'm a very fortunate man, Cassie. You have a kind and gentle way about you. I think we will get along very well."

Cassie lowered her gaze. "I will try not to disappoint you."

"I am sure you will not," he said, then reached out his hand as if to place it over hers, but pulled it back.

"There are several things I'd like to discuss with you before we reach Rosemont," he said.

"Ah," Cassie said on a teasing sigh. "You waited until now to tell me about the ghosts in the attic, or the mad aunt in the cellar."

"No," he said on a genuine laugh. "Nothing nearly so dramatic."

Her husband's eyes twinkled in amusement and the laughter in his voice remained for several moments. "I only want to warn you about the condition of Rosemont Manor. I'm afraid you will find several pieces of furniture in dire need of repair or replacement, and several of the rooms on the upper floors in need of paint and paper."

"In other words," she said, "you are telling me I will not find my life at Rosemont one of boredom and idleness."

"Why yes. That is exactly what I am saying."

Cassie met his gaze. "I appreciate your telling me and I look forward to having many busy days ahead of me. In fact, you had best pay close attention, or I may take a hammer to a perfectly fine wall just to add another project to my list. You see, I do love enlivening a décor." She smiled at the thought. "But I wonder, is there a limit to the amount I might spend to fix up our home?"

Quinn shook his head. "Thanks to your dowry, and your grandmother's generosity, there is no limit. She wanted to make sure the house you lived in was one you would be proud of, as well as comfortable in. If there is a limit on spending, the limit will be placed on me and what I spend on the grounds of the estate. But I don't see that happening anytime in the foreseeable future. The time will not be too far in the future before the farms on the estate earn their own way. With profits left over."

"Do you have a steward to oversee your lands?"

"Yes. He was hired by my father and has been with us for years. His name is Randolf Comstock. I rely on him for nearly everything connected to the land. I am trying to learn how to be a better manager, but Father and Robert took care of the estate. I joined the army before I had much experience in husbandry."

"As long as you have someone competent to oversee your properties, in time I'm sure you will learn all there is to know."

"I wish I had as much confidence in my abilities as you do," her husband said, giving her a heart-stopping smile.

Cassie was amazed at how at ease she felt around him. She had hoped that in time she would be comfortable with him, but she hadn't thought that camaraderie would happen this quickly. She hadn't thought she'd enjoy his company quite so much, or quite this soon.

They rode together a while longer and her husband told her about life at Rosemont Manor, about the new staff he'd hired to make the manor house presentable for a new mistress as well as Cook's name and the fact that her meals were incredibly good.

Then, he paused to point out the carriage window. "Do you see that large hedgerow to our right?"

Cassie looked to where he pointed. "Yes."

"That's the boundary line that separates Rosemont from our neighboring estate, Manford Park."

The carriage turned and Cassie watched as they passed through an opening in the hedgerow. "Oh, how marvelous. It's truly beautiful."

"I remember riding through this opening when I returned home. Both Father and Robert had been gone for several months and no one had been here to oversee the land. The hedgerow was overgrown and was barely clear enough for a rider to pass through, let alone a carriage. The first thing I did after moving in was to bring the two men who still remained at Rosemont here to clear the opening and trim the hedgerow."

"There were only two workers here?"

"The rest had moved on. With Father and Robert dead, they weren't getting paid. They needed to find other jobs to support their families."

"Oh," Cassie answered.

"Thankfully, shortly after I returned, I was able to hire a few more men and put them to work clearing the lane."

Before he could explain further, he leaned forward and pointed out the window.

"We're home. Welcome to Rosemont Manor, my lady."

Cassie leaned out the window and stared to where her husband pointed.

Her breath caught in her throat. She wasn't sure what she'd expected, but it wasn't a home as grand or massive as the enormous structure in front of her.

"Oh, Quinn. It's beautiful."

Quinn leaned back against the black velvet squabs and smiled. "I'm glad you approve, but I must warn you, both the interior and the façade are in desperate need of repair and redecorating."

"I happily accept the challenge, sir! It shall keep me busy."

Her husband smiled, then laughed. "I think you will never have to worry about not having enough to do, Lady Rosemont."

Cassie turned to look at her husband. This was the first time he'd called her by her title. It had rolled off his tongue so easily it was as if he'd called her that for years. It felt normal. As if the title fit.

Cassie watched out the window as the carriage pulled up before the front of the manor house. Four round pillars held up a white-railed portico. Several round flower beds, void of any living flowers, dotted the courtyard on either side of the cobbled circular drive. And the lawn was overgrown. A variety of weeds had taken over the area.

She vowed that one of her first tasks would be to hire a gardener to care for the lawn.

She walked into the house making a mental note to ask Quinn if he knew someone who could fill that position. If not, she was sure there was someone in the nearby town they could hire. Which reminded her to ask him where the nearest village was. They hadn't driven through any villages on their way here. Surely there was a town not too far away.

But the second Cassie entered the foyer, all coherent thought left her. She looked around the entryway to her new home in amazement. It was grand. What Quinn had told her had been correct. It was in need of a woman's touch. It would take more than a thorough cleaning to make it presentable. But she could imagine it as it would be when it was painted and polished. And the picture it presented was magnificent.

She turned to find her husband watching her, no doubt for her reaction. She smiled, then nodded her approval.

Only then did she realize that earlier she'd reached for his hand when he handed her out of the carriage and hadn't pulled away from his touch. And her back was still warm from his touch as he escorted her into the house. She hadn't pulled away from him. Nor had she panicked when he'd touched her.

This had not happened to her since that day five years ago when the man to whom she'd given her heart had left her at the altar.

She wondered if this calmness would continue, and she prayed it would.

CHAPTER SEVEN

Cassie couldn't have been happier seeing her new home. She wasn't at all disappointed. She'd half expected a home in greater need of repair. But other than lack of upkeep, it wasn't nearly as rundown as Quinn had led her to believe. Its bones were good, and that made all the difference.

She looked to the small queue of staff waiting to be introduced to their new mistress and smiled. She hoped her small gesture would endear her to the people waiting to meet her.

"Let me introduce you, my lady," her husband said.

He started at the front of the line and introduced her to the downstairs staff. There was Mrs. Rafferty, the housekeeper, and Betsy and Grace, the two maids.

"Thank you for making my new home so inviting, Mrs. Rafferty."

"You're welcome, my lady," the housekeeper said with a respectful curtsy.

Then there was Cook and her two kitchen helpers, her daughters, Daisy and Polly.

"It's a pleasure to meet you, Cook. I've heard nothing but glowing reports of your talent. I look forward to sampling your dishes. Especially your peach cobbler. His lordship says it's one of his favorites."

"Thank you, my lady," Cook said, wiping the flour from her

hands. "I've just taken some lemon biscuits from the oven. I'll send in a tray along with tea as soon as you're settled."

"Thank you very much. I have to admit I'm quite famished."

"Then, I'll make up a tray of sandwiches, too."

"That would be delightful," Cassie said with a smile. It seemed like forever since they'd last eaten.

Just then, a footman walked through the door carrying one of her trunks. Two more footmen followed with more of her belongings. They turned toward the grand staircase and carried the luggage up.

Before they'd gone out of sight, Cassie turned to the workers queued up before her. The staff was small, but by the look of her new home, seemed capable. Of course, the staff would have to be added to as improvements were made to the manor house and the newlyweds began to entertain.

"Thank you, all," she said to the gathering, then turned to Quinn and waited for him to lead her up the stairs.

"You are a natural," he said when they were out of hearing. "The staff is in love with you already."

"I'm not sure I'd say they are in love with me, but I think we got off on a good footing."

"I'd say you did," he said. "This is your suite of rooms," he said, opening a door in the center of the hallway.

Cassie walked into her room and looked around. "It's lovely," she said, then turned to look at her husband. "Thank you. For everything."

"My suite of rooms is next door."

Cassie nodded her approval.

"Even though we are not far from each other, you don't have to worry that I will intrude on your privacy. You can keep the inner door locked at all times." Quinn handed her a key. "And here is a key so you can keep the hall door locked to ensure your privacy. I assure you that you will be quite safe."

Cassie took the key and placed it in the pocket of her skirt. "Thank you, my lord."

He nodded. "Would you like to rest for a few moments, or—"

Cassie removed her bonnet and placed it on the bed. "No. Please, give me a few moments to freshen up. Then, I'd like to go to the nursery and meet your nieces, as well as introduce myself to Miss Portsmouth."

By his smile, Cassie knew she'd said the right thing. Making the little girls a priority over her own comfort seemed to please him immensely.

"Very well," he said. "I'll wait for you in the hall."

When Cassie was ready, she walked into the hall and Quinn escorted her to the third-floor nursery. Before they entered the room, Cassie heard the giggles of a child at play. Quinn opened the door and Cassie got her first look at the two little girls.

The older of the two was sitting on the floor with her legs stretched out before her. That would be Elizabeth, or as Quinn called her, Lizzy. She and Miss Portsmouth were rolling a ball back and forth on the floor.

The baby of five months was in a cradle, playing with a rattle and making an assortment of cooing sounds. That would be Molly. Every once in a while Miss Portsmouth would reach out and let the babe grab her finger, then she'd give the cradle a push so it would rock back and forth.

The sight of the two children was precious to behold. They seemed extremely happy and content. Cassie couldn't have been more touched.

She thought of the day when there might be more children in the nursery. Her children.

She'd always dreamed of having a house filled with children. Of a house echoing with laughter and children at play. She knew that came from growing up alone, of desperately wanting a brother or sister to talk to, play with. Simply to be there to share happy memories, or even sad ones.

Her father tried his best to give Cassie as much time as he could allow, but he was such a busy man it was difficult to find time from his duties as Earl of Granville.

Cassie turned her gaze to where the Earl of Rosemont stood and wondered what he thought of having more children. They hadn't discussed it before they married, but surely he wouldn't have any objections. He was, after all, an earl and would no doubt want to provide an heir. Since his brother had only had daughters, there was no one to pass the Rosemont title to. That would be his responsibility. So, hopefully, she could expect to have at least one child or two if her first child was a daughter.

She watched the three of them interact for a moment or two without being noticed. Only when she turned her head did the nursemaid see her and Quinn observing them. She paused. That was when Cassie got her first glimpse of Miss Portsmouth.

Her hair was a deep mahogany, and her eyes were a dark brown that glittered with laughter when she played with little Lizzy.

"Miss Portsmouth," Quinn said as he ushered Cassie into the room. "Allow me to present my wife, Lady Rosemont. Cassie, allow me to present Miss Chloe Portsmouth."

"How do you do, Miss Portsmouth?" Cassie greeted. "I've heard so much about you. I couldn't wait to meet you and Quinn's nieces."

"My best wishes to you on your marriage, Lady Rosemont. It's a pleasure to meet you. And this," she said bringing Lizzy out from where she was hiding behind her skirts, "is Lady Elizabeth Beckham."

Miss Portsmouth waited a moment, then asked Lady Elizabeth, "How do you greet a lady, Elizabeth?"

The five-year-old bobbed an unsteady curtsy, then said, "How do you do, Lady Rosemont?"

Cassie returned the child's curtsy, then crouched down so she was eye level with the little girl. "How do you do, Lady Elizabeth? I'm so glad to finally meet you."

"Are you married to my Uncle Quinn?"

"Yes, I am."

"Does that make you my aunt?"

"I suppose it does," Cassie said with a smile. "Does that meet with your approval?"

"I don't know. What does pa…rooval mean?"

"Well, approval means…is it all right with you that I'm your aunt?"

"Yes, I guess it is." She turned her head and looked at Quinn. "Do you want her to be my aunt, Uncle Quinn?"

"Yes, I think that would be an excellent idea."

"All right," she said. "You can be my aunt. And Molly's, too."

"Is Molly your sister?"

"Yes, she's here in this cradle. She doesn't know how to walk, so Miss Portsmouth lets her lie in her bed. She sleeps a lot and Miss Portsmouth says she's not old enough to play yet. She says she'll be more fun to play with when she can walk."

"I'm sure she will," Cassie answered. "Perhaps I can come to play with you until your sister can walk?"

"I'd like that," she answered, bobbing her dark curls. "Miss Portsmouth is teaching me how to serve tea. We have tea parties. Do you know how to serve tea?"

"Actually, I do."

"Is that because you're a lady? Uncle Quinn says every lady needs to know how to serve tea."

"Your Uncle Quinn is correct."

"I know. He's really clever," she whispered, loud enough that everyone could hear.

"Oh, I can tell he is."

"That's enough, Lizzy," Quinn said. "Perhaps you should introduce Molly to your new aunt."

"Would you like to meet my sister?"

"I'd love to."

"She can't talk yet, so she won't be able to say anything."

"That's all right. You can do the talking for her."

"All right," Lizzy said, then took Cassie's hand and led her to the cradle where the five-month-old lay.

Cassie was in love. Little Lizzy was the sweetest little girl she'd ever met. And she was as clever as she could be. Cassie couldn't wait to spend time with her and teach her all the things she would need to know.

Cassie recalled having tea parties with her mother before she passed away. They were always so much fun: Cassie's mother would tell her to watch closely so she would see how it was done, then she would pour two cups of tea. She always added one lump of sugar to her cup, and two lumps to Cassie's. Then she would place a confection on a plate and set it before Cassie, and take one for herself.

While they drank their tea, her mother would talk about all sorts of grown-up things, like what Lady Frandlin wore to the last ball Mother had attended and what she thought of her gown.

"Oh, Cassie. Lady Frandlin wore the most horrid puce gown imaginable. It didn't help her complexion one bit."

"What's puce, Mama?"

"It's a color, Cassie. The most pathetic shade of dark red you can imagine."

"Is knowing this important, Mama?"

"No, Cassie. It is not important."

"Then why are we talking about the color of Lady Frandlin's gown?"

"Because it is the hostess's duty to keep the conversation going so there is not a lag. If there is, your guests will get bored."

"Oh," Cassie answered.

But her favorite times were when she and her mother would go for walks in the garden. They would hold hands and stroll down the garden paths, then stop at one of the benches and watch the swans and the ducks swim by. This was so relaxing.

She would make sure she created memories just like that for Lizzy and Molly. She wanted them to have memories they would cherish for a lifetime.

Lizzy took her to the cradle where the baby lay.

"This is Molly. Her real name is Emmaline, but we call her Molly. Just like my real name is Elizabeth, but everybody calls me Lizzy."

"Then I will call you Lizzy, too. And you may call me Cassie."

"All right. I like that. I'll call you Aunt Cassie."

Cassie held out her hand and the babe grabbed her finger. She had a strong, healthy grip.

"Would you like to hold her?" Lizzy asked. "She loves to be held. Miss Portsmouth lets me hold her sometimes."

"Lizzy, I don't think she wants—" Quinn started to say.

"I would love to hold Molly," Cassie interrupted. Then she leaned over and lifted the babe out of her cradle. Cassie held her close and tucked the blanket around her to keep her warm.

Cassie was consumed by a motherly emotion. It wasn't unusual for her to make her way to the nursery when she visited her closest friend, Miss Genevieve Landsmore. She had five brothers and sisters and there was always a baby in their nursery. Genevieve always teased Cassie because what she thought of as an enjoyment, Genevieve considered punishment – having to watch over her siblings. Cassie would always gravitate to the smallest of the children and hold them, and play with them.

Cassie nestled little Molly next to her, then looked up to find Quinn standing close by. The emotion on his face was one of complete satisfaction. He smiled and Cassie returned his smile.

After a brief contact, she lowered her gaze.

"Do you like biscuits, Lizzy?" Cassie asked.

"Oh, yes. I love biscuits."

"Well, Cook informed me she just took some biscuits out of the oven. Would you like to join us for some biscuits and tea?"

"Can I?"

"May I?" Cassie gently corrected the little girl.

"May I?" Lizzy repeated.

"Yes, you may. Take your Uncle Quinn's hand and lead the way down the stairs to the drawing room."

Lizzy scampered to Quinn and reached for his hand. She was so excited that she couldn't stand still. "I get to go downstairs and have biscuits and tea with you," she said, moving constantly.

"So you do," Quinn said. "But you must be very careful and not spill your tea."

"I won't spill. I promise."

"Come, then," he said and took Lizzy's hand.

Cassie looked at Quinn, but he hadn't moved.

"You are remarkable," he said.

Cassie lowered her gaze. "I am hardly remarkable. Your nieces are the ones who are remarkable. They are very special."

"Yes, they are. But so are you."

They left the room and Cassie walked down the stairs with the babe in her arms and Quinn and Lizzy at her side.

They took tea in the morning room. Cassie couldn't remember a time she'd enjoyed more. She kept the conversation moving, just as her mother had taught her, and Lizzy added to the topic whenever she could. But the most impressive part of their afternoon was that Lizzy didn't spill her tea. Not one drop.

Miss Portsmouth joined them, but sat quietly to the side. When Molly grew tired, and Lizzy had consumed enough tea and biscuits, Miss Portsmouth took the girls back to their rooms.

"Can we have tea again, Cassie?" Lizzy asked before they left.

"Of course, Lizzy. There's nothing I would enjoy more."

"Oh, good," she exclaimed as she nearly skipped out of the room.

"You are amazing, Cassie," Quinn said when they were alone. "You are the best woman I could have married to help me with my nieces."

"They are easy to enjoy and spend time with. I'm glad they will be part of my world."

"So am I," Quinn said. "I'm ever so glad you will be a part of my world."

Cassie lifted her head and her gaze locked with Quinn's. She felt as though she could drown in the depth of his gaze.

Her cheeks warmed and she turned her head so Quinn wouldn't notice how much his words affected her. But they had.

IN TIME, CASSIE settled into a routine. She rose every morning to eat breakfast with Quinn and talk over their plans for the day. Then, the land steward, Randolf Comstock, would arrive and he and Quinn would leave for their morning ride over the property and discuss any changes and improvements that needed to be made.

While Quinn was gone, Cassie would speak with Mrs. Rafferty about areas that needed attention. She also asked her advice on new hires. It didn't take long to have a full staff in place for a house this large as well as a full kitchen staff.

Next, Cassie stopped in the kitchen to see what Cook was serving that day. The only time she made any changes to Cook's menu was when Lizzy or Quinn indicated there was something special they'd like to eat. Otherwise, Cassie always took Cook's suggestions, which she found most satisfactory.

On this particular morning, Cassie met Randolf Comstock coming from the kitchen. He didn't see her at first and Cassie got a close look at the man who oversaw the estate. He was quite a handsome man with dark hair and midnight blue eyes.

This morning he wore a broad smile. Cassie wondered who in the kitchen had caused such a grin.

"Good morning, Mr. Comstock," Cassie greeted when the land steward noticed her in front of him.

"Good morning, my lady."

"Is there something I can help you with?"

"Yes, my lady. I came to see his lordship."

"Is there a problem?"

"Yes. A stream that runs through a parcel of farmland has overflowed its banks."

"I see. Please wait here. I'll get his lordship."

Cassie went into the breakfast room where Quinn sat at the table just finishing his breakfast. He smiled as he rose.

"Good morning, my lady."

"Good morning, my lord. Your land steward needs to speak with you. He's waiting in the hall. Should I ask him to come in?"

"Yes, if you don't mind me discussing business while you eat."

"Not at all."

Cassie stepped out of the room and returned with Mr. Comstock.

"Please, Comstock. Have a seat. Have you eaten?"

"Yes, I came in through the kitchen and Cook was kind enough to feed me."

"Please, then," Quinn said. "Have a seat and tell me what is wrong."

Comstock sat where Quinn indicated, then explained the problem.

Cassie had only met Comstock once before and had been impressed with his knowledge of farming practices and animal raising. She could see why Quinn had kept him on to oversee the estate.

"Could you take some stable hands and dig some trenches to reverse the flow of the water?" Quinn wondered.

"I think that will work," Comstock answered. "Unless the water continues downstream at such a rate that we can't reroute the stream."

"We'll find out soon enough."

"That we will."

"I'll be out to help straightaway. I was going to work on the books, but that can wait."

"Might I be of help?" Cassie asked when she saw how desperately Quinn wanted to go with Comstock instead of being cooped indoors. "Not with rerouting the stream, of course, but with the ledgers. I used to assist my father all the time."

"Are you sure, Cassie?"

"Yes, more than sure. Taking care of the account ledgers was something I was quite good at when my father was alive. He taught me how to take care of the books, and left me to it when he was out overseeing the land."

"Am I taking you away from your scheduled activities of the day?"

"All I had planned was to have luncheon with Lizzy and Molly, and I can still do that. I'll take a break from working on the ledgers and have a meal with them, then continue with the ledgers when they take their naps."

"If you're sure you don't mind," Quinn said giving her a hopeful look.

"Not at all. In fact I'm looking forward to having something productive to do."

"Then, I thank you more than I can say," Quinn said. "I'll put the ledgers in your capable hands."

Cassie smiled at her husband, then sat down to eat her breakfast before going to Quinn's study. She was very pleased with the prospect of a new project and would happily tend to it first.

Quinn focused his gaze on her when Comstock left. "Thank you for helping with the bookkeeping. I've added and re-added the columns a dozen times and the numbers don't reconcile. Thank you for your offer."

"Not at all. I'm glad I can be useful."

"Everything should still be open on the desk. I don't know when I'll be back."

Cassie watched Quinn leave the room, then finished her tea and went to the study. She sat down with a sense of satisfaction. She was glad she could be of some use.

She was especially glad her father had taught her how to keep their estate's accounts.

She knew not many women were taught the business side of estates, but her father wasn't so narrow-minded. He was always of the mindset that every woman should know how their estate worked so if the day ever came when she was left alone to manage the estate, she could not be taken advantage of.

Besides, this would give her more to do, and for the first time she felt she could be a valuable asset to her husband.

CHAPTER EIGHT

"Do you have plans for the day?" Quinn asked over breakfast the following morning.

Cassie looked up from the food on her plate and shook her head. "No, nothing special. Do you have something in mind?"

"Yes," he said with a sly look on his face. "I'd like you to accompany me."

"Accompany you?"

"Yes. I'm in the mood for a picnic."

Cassie placed her fork beside her plate and looked at him. "A picnic?"

"Yes. The sun is shining and there's a place I'd like to show you. One of my favorite places on the estate."

Cassie couldn't stop the excitement from building inside her. "I'd love to," she answered.

"Good. You haven't had a chance to ride your new horse, and I thought this would be a perfect day for you to become acquainted with her."

Cassie's heart raced in her breast. "Just give me a few moments to change and I'll be right down."

Quinn slid his chair away from the table and rose. "At least finish your tea. I'll ask Cook to prepare a picnic lunch."

Cassie quickly finished her tea, then rose. She ran up the stairs and changed into her houndstooth riding habit. She fixed her hair in a low knot that would allow her riding hat to sit neatly in place. Pleased with the result, she tugged on her boots and hurried back downstairs to find Quinn waiting in the foyer with a blanket in one hand and a basket in the other.

"Are you ready?"

"Yes! I feel like I've just woken up and it's my birthday!"

Quinn stopped walking. "You know," he said, looking at her with a quizzical expression. "I don't know when your birthday is."

Cassie laughed. "It's several months from now. In the autumn. And I don't know when your birthday is, either."

"Winter. I can't tell you how many years my birthday party had to be postponed due to snow."

"We'll have to plan celebrations for each," she said, "And I'll be sure to factor in the snow!"

She reached for the blanket to have something to carry.

"That's an excellent idea," he answered and took her arm to escort her out the door to the two horses waiting for them.

"She's beautiful, Quinn. Have I told you how grateful I am to you?"

A smile lit his face. "Several times. What have you named her?"

"I've called her Comet."

"Comet?" he said. "Is there a reason you've called her Comet?"

"Yes. Because I expect her to race like a star shooting through the nighttime sky."

He laughed. "And what if she's as slow as molasses?"

Cassie cast him a look over her shoulder. "She won't be. She and I had a long conversation where I explained to her the reason I named her Comet. She told me she understood the meaning of her name and promised me she'd do her name proud."

"She did? She told you that?"

"Yes, she did."

Quinn put his arm around her shoulders and pulled her close

to him. Cassie didn't shy away from him, but instead went to him willingly.

"Oh, Quinn, you have a sidesaddle for me. Is it your mother's? Did your mother ride?"

"Like the wind," he smiled, clearly liking the memory of it. "We would race over the hills nearly every day."

He laughed heartily. It was the most magical sound she'd ever heard.

"Mostly, she did. If I won, it was because she let me."

"How old were you?"

"Not yet ten."

"You've improved a great deal since then. I think she would have a difficult time beating you now."

"No doubt, but I would love to see her face when I let her win."

Cassie looked at the longing in Quinn's eyes and experienced a clutching of her heart. The man her grandmother chose for her was indeed very special.

They mounted and Cassie rode beside Quinn down the lane and through a meadow. She heard the rushing water before she saw the stream and pushed her horse to go faster.

"Oh, Quinn," she said when she reached the bank of the brook. She stopped Comet and took in the area around her. "It's beautiful. Simply beautiful."

"I knew you'd like it," he said, dismounting, then stepping over to help her to the ground. "This was always one of my favorite places on the estate."

"I can see why. It's so peaceful here."

"Would you like to eat first or go for a walk?"

"Let's walk. I need to work up an appetite. It's too beautiful a day to stay sitting in one spot."

Quinn smiled at her then reached for her hand and hooked her arm through his. They left the blanket and the basket on the ground and started to walk down a narrow path opposite the rippling water.

"It looks as if someone comes here often. They've worn a path near the stream."

"That would be me. I come here when I need to think."

"And you need to think so often?" she teased.

He smiled down on her. "Not as much since I met you, Cassie. I wanted to bring you here so I could explain how much I appreciate everything you've done for me. And for the girls. They both adore you."

"I adore them, too."

"I know you do. It's obvious by how much time you spend with them, and how you interact with them. I saw you yesterday when you strolled through the garden. Lizzy skipped down the path ahead of you, and you were pushing Molly in her pram. You made an endearing sight."

"I love the out of doors and the girls do too. I want to take them out as much as possible. At least until winter comes."

"I worry sometimes, though," he said as they made their way along the path beside the stream, "about how hesitant you were to marry. That it was something you never wished to do."

Cassie didn't answer Quinn and continued taking steps down the path.

"Your grandmother told me you had a disastrous experience with a man you wanted to marry, a man you thought you loved. Was that the reason you did not want to consider marriage?"

Cassie contemplated how much she wanted to reveal to her husband, then decided she needed to be brutally honest with him. Honesty was a quality that was essential in any marriage.

"Yes. I met the Marquess of Weatherly during my first Season and fell head over heels in love. He was everything I'd dreamed of in a suitor. He was kind and attentive, and had a wonderful sense of humor. He had an admirable title and was exceedingly well-liked. There was always a crowd around him, and he had a marvelous way about him."

"And he was handsome," Quinn filled in for her.

"Yes. He was extremely handsome. I thought I was the most

fortunate woman in London when he chose me to be his bride.

"What I didn't know was that he'd previously courted Lady Penelope Dolman and her father had forced their courtship to end when he arranged her marriage to the son of his long-time friend.

"I'd heard rumors, of course, but I refused to believe them. I was in love and I thought he was, too. I was unbelievably happy when he asked me to marry him and dove into planning my wedding.

"And then, the day came. I woke early and spent hours getting ready. The church was overflowing with lilacs, so many you could smell them as you approached, and there was a multitude of guests, so many that some could not even fit in the church. I couldn't wait for everyone I'd invited to see me walk down the aisle.

"It was a perfect day. The organ was playing, and everyone was looking around in anticipation. But the groom didn't arrive.

"At first I thought he was simply late, but after fifteen minutes turned into a half hour, and that half hour neared an hour, I realized my groom wasn't going to come.

"That day was the most humiliating day of my life. Eventually, my uncle told the congregation to go home, that there would be no wedding. I didn't think I'd ever survive that embarrassment, but thanks to my grandmama, I did. She refused to allow me to wallow in self-pity like I wanted to. She only gave me a small amount of time before she forced me to get back to living."

Quinn wrapped his arm more tightly around her in an effort to comfort her.

"That is why I was hesitant to marry. I swore that day I would never trust my heart to another man as long as I lived."

"Do you still feel that way?"

Cassie stopped walking and turned to face Quinn. She tried to smile but knew her smile did not reach her eyes. "That is a moot point, Quinn, since we are already married, and I did not have to fear that you would leave me waiting at the altar."

"No, I did not leave you. And I never would. I want to make you a promise, Cassie. I know how much courage it took for you to marry me, just as I know it will take even more courage for you to trust me with your heart. But in time, I hope I can earn your trust. I will do everything in my power to be worthy of you."

"Oh, Quinn," Cassie said. Her eyes filled with tears that threatened to spill down her cheeks. "That is all I can ask of you."

"For now, all that is important is that you learn to trust me to take care of you and be there when you need me."

"Quinn," she whispered as his mouth came down on hers.

His kiss was passionate yet tender, filled with desire and need. Cassie returned his kiss with unexpected eagerness.

She'd never been kissed like this. Never had so much asked of her, demanded from her.

She wrapped her arms around Quinn's neck and returned his kiss with the mere bit of restraint she could summon. His passion was evident. His desire obvious. And she wished to give him what he asked from her. As much as she dared.

He kissed her several times and brought her up against him as if he feared he might lose her.

Cassie pressed herself against him to answer his pleas, then drew her fingers through his hair as he sought to deepen the kiss.

The heart she was hesitant to give away was no longer hers to keep. Somehow, without her realizing it, Quinn had stolen it from her breast and tucked it next to his own.

She'd promised herself she would never give her heart away to any man, yet that's exactly what she was doing. She was giving her heart away to a man who couldn't promise to keep it safe. The very work he did, the risks he took on every mission he was assigned, might prevent him from keeping his promise.

She remembered his words. The vow he'd made to always put his work first and his family second. That meant he intended to put the work he did for the government ahead of her, ahead of his nieces, ahead of any children they might have together.

She must never forget that. She must never give him so much of her heart that she couldn't survive with the small part that was left. She would die without enough of her heart left to keep her body alive.

He kissed her once more, then lifted his head. "I fear I've let you into my heart, Cassie."

"Have you?"

"Yes, I have."

"And you didn't intend to?"

"Not intentionally."

"But neither did I intend to keep you out."

Cassie lifted her hand and cupped his cheek. "Neither did I, Quinn. I think it just happened."

"Yes, it just happened."

"Is that because of the work you do for the government?"

Quinn dropped his arm from around her. "How much do you know about what I do for the government?"

"Only what you've told me. I know the government sends you on assignments" Cassie took a step away from Quinn and looked him in the eyes. "Are you a spy?"

All at once, Cassie felt that she knew exactly what her husband did. Why else would the government send him on assignments other than to find information they needed or go undercover to steal something they needed? "Are you?"

"Would it bother you if I were?"

"You are," she said as the reality of what her husband did for the government settled over her. "Is the work you do for the government dangerous?"

Quinn smiled at her, then pulled her back in his arms and held her close. "No, what I do is not dangerous. Not at all. At the height of the war it was a little more exciting. But not now. The war is over so there is no more danger."

"Then, what do you do?"

"Mostly, I go where they send me and keep watch for anything that's going on, Then, I go back and report what I saw.

"That's all?"

"That's all," he answered. He lowered his head and kissed her forehead then pressed his finger beneath her chin and lifted her head until their gazes locked. "See, I told you I don't do anything dangerous. Now, put this out of your mind. I don't want you to give my work another thought."

Cassie forced a smile. "If you say so,"

"I do."

But what he said was a lie. Cassie knew it was. His work was much more dangerous than he let on.

HE TURNED HER in his arms and draped his arm across her shoulders. He kept her close to him as they made their way along the brook's bank. They turned at the end of the lane and returned to where they'd left their blanket and basket of food.

Cassie played back the conversation they'd just had as well as the emotions they'd provoked. She let her gaze rest on his features, the strong lines and angles of his high cheekbones. The firm cut of his jaw. He was all strength and commanding power. Cassie couldn't deny that he was blindingly handsome, but his handsome features weren't what drew her to him. That would be the goodness and decency that lay inside him. That would be the integrity that defined his character.

Cassie tried to remember the first time she'd seen him after their accident. The moment she saw him standing in her bedroom doorway. The exact second their eyes locked, and she realized that he was someone special. That the man her grandmother was bringing to her was someone whose qualities were remarkable. She remembered what her grandmother said when she asked her why she'd chosen him to be her husband, and she said it was because he reminded her of her husband, Matthew. Quinn had reminded the dowager countess of the love of her life, and she wanted Cassie to experience that same eternal love she had known.

Cassie knew the foundation for a long and lasting love had

been forged the first time they'd looked at each other. She didn't doubt that her feelings for him had grown stronger as she came to know him. Just as she knew without a doubt that she had fallen in love with him.

Cassie readied the lunch while Quinn spread the blanket beneath a large shade tree, then she sat beside him and handed him a plate of food.

"I'm glad you thought of this," she said as they ate the ham and cheeses Cook had sent, along with the assortment of fresh breads and jams.

Quinn filled two tumblers with a dark, sweet wine and they drank one, then couldn't resist another.

"What do you think now, my lord?" Cassie said putting the food back into the basket. "Should we return home?"

Cassie needed to be alone. She needed to think. She needed to decide what path she should take to protect her heart from being destroyed by her love for her husband. Because, she knew now that she loved him. And if something happened to him, his loss would destroy her.

"I should think not," he answered, pulling her close to him and taking her with him to lie on the blanket. "It's a perfect day to take a well-deserved nap beneath a shade tree."

Cassie couldn't help but smile at him. He was right. It was a perfect day for a nap. And more.

Cassie wasn't sure where that thought came from. She had no intention of giving herself to Quinn, yet there was an ache inside her breast that yearned for her to give herself to him just once. The prospects of a long, quiet marriage had changed dramatically when she discovered he chose the excitement and risks he took for the government over the quiet and staid life of a country farmer. That he would rush to battle every time he was called frightened her to death, because she knew the day would come when he would come home in a coffin, or on a stretcher.

Cassie already knew she could not live that kind of life, with that kind of worry lurking around every corner. The longer she stayed with him, the more she would come to love him, and the more terrified she would become that she would lose him.

And yet, she was desperate to love him just once. She needed to have one memory of them together that she could cherish in her lifetime without him. Just one. Surely a child would not be the result of making love just one time.

It wasn't that she did not want Quinn's child, it was only that she did not dare to bring another child into his world. He might think he could protect her and be there when she needed him, but he could not. Not if she came in second in his life and the work he did for the government came first. She could never accept that reality.

Cassie lay on the blanket beneath the broad shade tree and Quinn came down over her. He looked at her and the expression on his face changed. It turned more serious. More determined.

He lowered his head and kissed her with all the passion he'd kissed her with before.

"Make love to me, Quinn," she whispered. "Just this once."

"Are you sure?"

"I'm sure."

He leaned over her and kissed her again. While he kissed her, he worked at the fastenings of her riding habit until Cassie felt the warm sunshine and a soft breeze against her flesh.

Quinn deepened his kiss and Cassie matched his desire. Then, he made her his wife in the true sense of the word.

CHAPTER NINE

EVERYTHING CHANGED BETWEEN Quinn and Cassie after their time together by the stream. Cassie felt a growing hope that they could be a family. As if her fear that she would always come in second to Quinn's obligations to his country was only a fantasy. That if the time ever came for him to choose between her and a mission he'd been chosen to go on, he would choose her. That his love for her was powerful enough for him to make the right choice in the end.

She promised to do everything in her power to be a wife to him in all things. To help him wherever she could.

Between making time to be with the girls and taking a few minutes each day to check in with Cook and Mrs. Rafferty, she always managed to spend an hour or two working on the estate ledgers.

The more time she spent with Quinn, the better she knew him. He was a natural leader, which was why he'd achieved the rank of colonel in the army. He was also level-headed and worked extremely hard to accomplish whatever he set out to do. And the better she got to know him, the more impressed she was with the man she'd married.

Somewhere, in the back of her mind, she thought that even though Quinn told her his work with the government was too important to him to give up, she was convinced that she and the girls had become so important that he wouldn't be able to give them up. That when the time came, he would choose his family over his work with the government.

They sat together each night after they put the girls to sleep and talked. She shared everything with him. There wasn't anything he didn't know about her, and she didn't think there was anything she didn't know about him. There weren't secrets between them, and Cassie felt as though she was closer to him than she was to anyone.

They shared a bed each night and they made love. He told her over and over that he loved her, and his words were sincere. She didn't doubt that he meant every word he spoke.

And then, she realized his words were a lie. She understood that he said only what he knew she wanted to hear. That he hadn't meant any of the words he'd said.

One afternoon, Cassie was deep in her work with the ledgers when Quinn entered the room.

She looked up and saw that he was dressed to travel.

"Are you going somewhere?"

"Yes, I've been called away."

Her heart fell to the pit of her stomach. "Where?" she asked.

"I…I'm not sure."

Cassie rose from her chair and walked around the desk until she faced him. "You're not sure, or you can't say?"

"I can't say, Cassie. Don't ask."

"I see."

She wasn't sure why she reacted as she did, but she reached out and clasped his hands as if she could keep him from leaving.

"Will you be in danger?"

A broad grin crossed his face. "No, my love. I won't be in danger."

"How long will you be gone?"

"I'm not sure. I should be back in a couple of days."

"Are you going alone—?"

"Cassie," he warned.

"I'm being silly, aren't I?"

"Yes. There's nothing to worry about. It's just a little trip. I'll be back in a few days."

"If I asked you to stay—"

The expression on his face hardened. He was suddenly far removed from her. "Cassie, don't. You know I don't have a choice. This is what I do. It's what I've given my promise to do."

Cassie opened her mouth to remind him of another promise, but before she could utter another word, Quinn's valet appeared in the doorway with a satchel. "You're ready, my lord."

"Thank you, Hodgkins."

"I've got to go now," Quinn said, clasping his fingers around her arms and pulling her toward him. "Don't worry," he said, lowering his mouth and kissing her.

"Of course," she answered, although the look on his face said he knew her words for the lies they were.

Without another word of reassurance, he turned and left her.

Cassie stood by the window until he was out of sight.

Was this how things would be for the rest of their lives? Would he be summoned to leave on a moment's notice, and she be left behind, not knowing if he would return?

Cassie wasn't sure she was strong enough to survive that kind of life. Especially now that her heart was more his than hers. Especially if she let herself care for him as if she couldn't survive without him. That wasn't part of the bargain she'd made with him. That wasn't one of the stipulations to their marriage, was it? Yet...

Yes, it was.

He'd told her from the start that he couldn't give up his work for the government. He'd told her it was too important for him to turn his back on his country. On his work.

Cassie thought back to that day at her grandmother's. He'd laid out the benefits to their marriage, as well as the drawbacks. The benefits for her were that she would never be threatened by either of her uncles to hand over control of her money. She would never be controlled by either of them, nor forced to marry someone she could not tolerate.

Cassie walked away from the window and returned to the chair behind her desk. The solution was simple. If she wanted to avoid getting hurt, there was only one answer to her problem. She had to make sure she never allowed herself more than a companionable love.

How she might manage that she hadn't a clue—because any fool could see she was deeply in love with the man. She could only pray he might stay away long enough for her to get a grip on her heart and convince herself that she didn't love him as deeply as she did.

CASSIE FOUND THAT the days progressed with agonizing slowness while she waited for Quinn to return from wherever he was. She tried to convince herself that the mission on which he was sent wasn't dangerous, but she failed miserably. She could imagine him injured and bleeding in a roadside ditch. Or worse yet, dead. And he'd left her absolutely no information as to where she might make inquiries whether he was even still alive.

Keeping busy was the only way she could keep her mind from imagining the worst, so she rose early every morning and after breaking her fast, she met with Randolf Comstock to get a briefing on events concerning the estate. Then, she checked in with Cook and Mrs. Rafferty. She went through any problems either of them had and did her best to solve them.

After that, she went to the nursery and took her luncheon with Lizzy and Molly.

"When is Uncle Quinn coming back?" Lizzy asked when Quinn had been gone several weeks.

"I don't know, Lizzy. He didn't know how long he would be gone."

"I miss him," she complained.

"I know sweetling. I miss him, too."

"Did you get angry with him?" she asked. "Is that why he left?"

"No, I didn't get angry with him. Why would you think I was angry with him?"

"Because you aren't as happy as you used to be."

Cassie smiled, then held Lizzy's hand. At the same time, she held out her hand and Molly clutched her finger. She pushed on Molly's finger and her cradle moved back and forth.

"If I'm not as happy as I used to be, it's because I miss your Uncle Quinn."

"I do, too," Lizzy said. "When we go to bed tonight I think we should ask God to send him home."

Cassie smiled. "I think that's a wonderful idea, Lizzy." Cassie and Lizzy finished their luncheon, then she waited until Miss Portsmouth prepared the girls for their nap.

She couldn't believe how they were growing, and how comfortable they were with her. It had only been a few months since she'd arrived, yet it seemed like she'd been a part of their lives forever.

While the girls napped, Cassie worked on the estate books. When the girls woke from their naps, some days she took them for a walk around the gardens, or as far as to the stream where she and Quinn had picnicked.

She didn't go to the brook all that often though. It brought up memories she didn't want to relive. Memories of how special her time with Quinn had been beneath a certain shade tree.

Cassie ate alone every evening, then spent several hours in the library. Nights were the worst. The hours crept by at an alarmingly slow pace. Maybe it was because the house was quiet and she had more time to contemplate, but these hours were the longest. Her thoughts were more troubling, her fears more terrifying. Yet, the days crept by. One long agonizing day bled into another until it had been four weeks since Quinn had left her.

Four weeks on a trip he estimated would take a week at the most. Cassie couldn't keep the worry from eating away at her.

She knew she wasn't getting the sleep she needed. Neither was she eating enough. She was losing enough weight that her clothes would soon require altering and there was nothing she could do to prevent it. How could she eat when everything she put in her mouth threatened to come back up? How could she get the rest she needed when she couldn't sleep?

Cassie paced the floor, checking the windows for any sign that Quinn had returned. But the view to the front remained empty. She watched a few more minutes, then wrapped a heavy quilt around her shoulders and snuggled into a cushioned wing chair. She watched the fire in the fireplace until the flames died to embers. Sometime before the fire was out she fell asleep.

QUINN WAS SO exhausted he could barely stay atop his horse, but he was determined to make it home yet tonight. This mission wasn't supposed to take this long. It was a simple task to travel to London and meet another agent and bring back the plans for a minor uprising in France. Instead, what should have taken four or five days had taken more than four weeks with a trip across the Channel and a week undercover in Montpellier.

Quinn pushed Atlas until the horse was lathered and ready to give up. But, he was desperate to get home. He didn't want Cassie to have to worry about him one more night.

At last he reached Rosemont. His home had never looked so good. He'd never been so relieved in his life.

He entered the front door as quietly as he could, not wishing to wake any of the servants. He only wanted to sneak up the stairs and crawl into bed beside Cassie. But when he crossed the foyer, he noticed a light shining from the library.

He turned, then made his way down the hall until he reached the library. He walked quietly through the open library door and saw her.

Cassie was curled up in a cushioned chair as if waiting for him to return.

He walked to her and took in the sight. She looked peaceful and calm sleeping in the chair, but there were dark circles beneath her eyes that hadn't been there when he left a month ago. And her face was gaunt, as if she'd recently lost some weight.

Quinn knelt before her and reached for her hand. "Cassie?" he whispered. He didn't want to startle her.

"Cassie?" he repeated in a louder whisper.

She shifted beneath the blanket.

"Cassie?"

Her eyes fluttered, then opened.

At first her eyes were just narrow slits, then they opened wide and she sat up in surprise.

"Quinn?"

"Yes, sweetheart."

"Oh, Quinn," she said throwing her arms around his neck and wrapping him in a death grip. "You're home! You're safe!"

"Yes, I'm home and I'm safe." He pulled her against him and kissed her.

He kissed her several times and she returned his kisses with a desperation that frightened him. "Cassie?" He held her away from him and for the first time, he got a good look at her.

She was crying. Torrents of tears streamed down her face in massive rivers, dripping from her chin to dampen the front of her gown.

A sense of foreboding engulfed him. "Cassie? What's wrong?"

She shook her head. "Nothing. You're home. You're safe."

"Yes, I'm home and I'm safe."

Quinn stood and pulled her into his arms. That's when he realized how thin she'd become. How loosely her clothes hung on her body.

"What's wrong, Cassie? Have you been ill?"

"No, not at all. I'm fine."

Quinn clasped her upper arms and held her far enough away that he could look her in the eyes. "No, you're not. How long have you been ill? Since when?"

"Since when?" he asked again, when she didn't answer him the first time.

"Since you left!" she cried back at him. "Since you went away, and I didn't know if you were lying in a ditch somewhere injured or dead. Since you told me you'd only be gone a week at the most and it's been a month! Since for a whole month I was afraid you were dead, and I wasn't sure I could live the rest of my life without you! Since—"

Quinn pulled her against him and held her tight. "Shh, Cassie. Shh."

He wrapped his arms around her and nestled her to him as her body trembled with the racking sobs. Dear God, what had he put her through?

"Come," he said leading her to the nearest sofa and sitting with her. He held her as tenderly as if she might break at any moment. "Don't be afraid. Everything will be all right. I'm fine. I'll always be fine. I promise I will."

"You can't make that promise."

"I can. Cassie, listen to me. The missions they send me on are just diplomatic missions. There are no enemy lines to cross. I simply meet with other agents to retrieve missives that can't be sent by any other means. That can't be seen by anyone else."

This oversimplification made him wince a bit at the deception.

Quinn leaned over and kissed her forehead, then placed his finger beneath her chin and tilted her face upward. When she was close enough, he pressed his mouth to hers and kissed her.

The passion he felt was all-consuming. He'd fallen in love with her, even though he didn't think it was possible for him to love anyone. He never had.

Quinn had had his share of women. He was far from living the life of a monk. But he'd never been in love. Not really. So, the fact that he was in love with Cassie shocked him to his very core.

Ordinarily, he would have spent his days biding his time until he could return from a mission. But this time, all he could think about was Cassie and how desperate he was to get back to her. This time he pushed Atlas to go faster than was safe, because he couldn't get back to Cassie fast enough.

Quinn wasn't sure when it had happened, but Cassie was suddenly more important than his work for the government. She was becoming a priority where his work had always held that spot. And he knew the reason for his feelings.

He'd fallen in love with his wife.

He ended the kiss and lifted her to his lap. When she was settled, he kissed her again, then again. She drew back a bit and looked at him, then she tucked her head in the crook of his neck and nestled close.

"I was terrified I would never see you again."

"You can't worry like that, Cassie."

"How can I help but worry, Quinn? You can't guarantee that you will always return. It's not within your power to make such a promise."

Quinn wrapped his arms around her more securely and silently held her. He needed to give her time to calm, time to gain control of her emotions. The words he needed to speak to her weren't going to be easy for him to say or for her to hear. But they needed to be said, and they needed to be said now.

Although Cassie was becoming the most important part of his life, the work he did was still important. He wasn't ready to give it up. Cassie needed to understand that.

After several minutes, he spoke.

"Cassie, I need to speak with you. And it's important that you understand what I'm saying."

She shifted on his lap so she was able to look at him.

"I never thought this would happen," he began.

"What?"

"That I would fall in love with you."

"You've fallen in love with me?"

"Yes, silly. I've fallen in love with you. How could I not have? You're everything I could ask for in a wife. Everything I could want in a mother for Lizzy and Molly. You're perfect."

"Oh, Quinn."

"And, that's what makes what I have to say so very difficult."

"What do you have to say?"

"Do you remember what we agreed on before we married?"

She nodded with tears in her eyes. "You agreed that you would give me time before we made love, and I agreed that I would allow you to continue with the work you do for the government."

"Yes," he whispered.

"But that was before I fell in love with you. That was before I thought I would ever love you. But I love you now, Quinn. I couldn't bear the thought of losing you."

Quinn gently removed Cassie from his lap and rose. When he was on his feet, he walked to the liquor table and poured himself a glass of brandy. On legs that trembled beneath him, he made his way to the French doors and stared out into the darkness.

"Are you saying that you've changed your mind? That you can no longer live with what I do for the government?"

"I don't know," she said. Her voice was filled with agony. Her eyes held a faraway look brimming with raw hurt. There was more desperation in the expression on her face than he ever wanted to see. Especially on the face of the woman he loved.

"We have a decision to make then, don't we?"

"Yes," he heard Cassie whisper from behind him.

"What do you see as our options, Cassie?"

She didn't speak for several long moments. Finally, Quinn turned to face her. She didn't look at him, but instead lowered her gaze to stare at her hands clenched in her lap.

"I don't know," she finally answered.

"Surely, you have an idea as to what choices are open to us."

"There is only one option left me if you insist on working for the government. I will have to learn to live with the knowledge that you will leave me to go on missions whenever the government calls you to go. I can, perhaps, learn to live with that knowledge."

"And if you cannot?"

The color left her face, and she shook her head.

"I see." He answered her revelation with a whisper of defeat.

Quinn stared out into the darkness.

Cassie sat in silence for several long torturous moments.

Finally, she rose from her seat and walked away from him.

Without a word, she left the room...

And him.

✤

CHAPTER TEN

Cassie rose early the next morning and dressed with little assistance. When she felt ready to face the day, she went down the stairs and into the small breakfast room, thankful to find she would be alone.

She sat at the table and poured herself a cup of coffee and drank it, then poured herself a second cup. When she was on her third cup, a footman entered with serving dishes of rashers of bacon, eggs, sausage, and a platter of toasted bread. It wasn't long after that Quinn entered the room.

"Good morning, Cassie," he greeted and walked to the breakfast buffet.

"Good morning, Quinn."

He filled a plate with food, then brought it to the table and set it in front of her.

"I'm not hung—"

"Eat. You need to gain back the weight you've lost."

He returned to the buffet, filled a plate for himself, and sat down beside her. "Did you get any sleep?" he asked.

She shook her head and finished spreading jam on a piece of toast.

"Neither did I."

He put a forkful of food into his mouth, then watched her until she ate something from her plate. He didn't speak until she ate a second bite.

"I imagine you spent a great deal of time considering what we're going to do."

She lifted her gaze to meet his. "I've thought of little else."

"And what conclusion did you come to?"

She shook her head. "None. What did you decide?"

"Cassie," he said, reaching over and placing his hand atop hers. "I love you. You know that I do. But I also love my country and the work I do for the Crown."

He squeezed her fingers. "I can't give up that work."

A lump formed in her throat. "In other words, this decision is mine to make. You've already decided what you are going to do."

"It's what I have to do," he answered in a firm whisper.

Cassie kept her gaze focused on his, then slowly pulled her hand from beneath his. "Let me be sure I understand this. We can continue as we have been, living our lives as husband and wife, until you get word that your country needs you. Then, you will abandon us – me, Lizzy, and Molly – until your mission is completed."

"It's how it must be, Cassie. I thought you understood that from the beginning."

Cassie wrung her hands. "I did. I understood that even before we married. I just didn't think I would fall in love with you. I didn't think it would matter so much if I lost you."

Quinn stood and reached out to grab her hands. When she was on her feet, he pulled her to him and wrapped his arms around her and held her tight.

Cassie pressed her cheek against his chest and breathed in the scent of him, the unique smell of the outdoor and soap he used each morning.

"The missions I'm sent on are no more dangerous than some of the work I do on the estate."

"How can you say that? Of course they are more dangerous. The work you do on the estate does not take you into hostile areas. It doesn't force you to meet with characters who would rather you didn't return to England with what you've come to get. The missions you're sent on are much more dangerous and you know it."

"Ah, Cassie," he said, holding her close and rubbing his hands up and down her spine. "Just give us time. Give yourself time to adjust to what I do. In time you'll realize you have nothing to worry about."

Quinn placed his finger beneath her chin and lifted. When her gaze was locked with his, he brought his lips down to meet hers.

His kiss was filled with a depth of passion and caring that emphasized what he felt for her. He loved her as fully as she loved him, but he wasn't the one being forced to make all the sacrifices. He wasn't the one who risked losing her. She was the one risking everything. And she didn't think she could survive if she lost him.

He deepened his kiss and she welcomed it.

"I love you, Cassie," he said between kisses.

"And I love you, Quinn. More than I thought it was possible to love another human being."

"Give yourself time. Please. I can't lose you, Cassie. I'm not sure I could survive if you weren't beside me."

Quinn's words clenched at her heart more powerfully than a vice had clamped around it. Even though she fought the realization that screamed in her mind, the words refused to go away.

What was wrong with her? How could she be so selfish? This was who he was. A man who'd devoted his life to helping others. A man who lived by a code of honor. A man she should be proud to call her husband, instead of allowing him to believe she didn't see the worth in his actions.

How could she listen to him and doubt his words? How could she ignore the sincerity of his words? He had always been completely honest with her. He had never lied to her, and she knew he never would.

She loved Quinn as desperately as he loved her. How could

she be so foolish that she would risk losing the man who possessed her heart? She had promised to love, honor, and obey him. She had agreed to marry him, knowing full well that he had an obligation to the Crown. Knowing full well that what he did could possibly save thousands of lives?

How could she put her feelings above the lives of innocent citizens when she'd known, even before she married him, what he expected of her?

Cassie raised her hand and cupped Quinn's cheek. Her heart ached with the love she felt for him. "I can't lose you either, Quinn. I couldn't survive if you weren't here at my side. I'm sorry I was so selfish. I know how important what you do for the government is to you and I won't stand in your way. I'm proud of you. I'm proud of what you do. Never doubt that."

"Oh, Cassie. How did I get so lucky to find you?"

Cassie smiled. "You didn't find me. I found you, and it almost cost me my life."

Quinn lowered his head and kissed her.

"But it was worth it," Cassie said, then wrapped her arms around his neck and deepened their kiss.

IT HAD BEEN a little more than three weeks since Cassie had assured him she would never leave him. Nearly a month since she told him he wouldn't lose her. But he wasn't ready to test her resolve. Not yet. He woke up every day fearing that another missive would come, and he'd be ordered on another mission.

Everything between them seemed better than ever. They settled back into their routine as if nothing had threatened their marriage. Cassie spent time with Lizzy and Molly, then worked on the estate books, while he rode the land with his steward or supervised repairs in the grain sheds or made plans for next year's planting season. Everything seemed to be running smoothly.

But Quinn knew it was only a matter of time until his peaceful world would be tested, and he wanted to do something before that happened.

"Are you still working on those books?" he asked, entering the study to find her busy behind his desk.

"Yes, but I was about to finish. Did you need something?"

"Yes. I need to make a trip to London. I have some estate business to take care of and I wondered if you would like to come with me."

Her eyes lit up and a smile crossed her face.

"How long would we be gone?"

"I think no longer than four or five days. A week at the most."

"Oh, yes, Quinn. There's nothing I'd like more. I'm so looking forward to seeing Grandmama. We could stay with her. I'm sure she wouldn't mind."

"Mind?" he said on a chuckle. "You know as well as I do that she'd be insulted if we stayed anywhere else."

"Yes. You're right."

Cassie was on her feet and heading for the door. "When do you want to leave?"

"Can you be ready first thing in the morning?"

"Oh, yes! I'll be ready."

"Perfect."

"I'll go up and tell Leann to pack."

Cassie raced for the door but stopped short of it to turn and face him. "Thank you," she said and left.

Quinn felt as if he'd done something to repair any strife between them. He knew she'd been worried about her grandmother, and this was a perfect opportunity to see her. It was also a perfect chance for him to meet with Theo and Jack. He wasn't sure why, but he thought if Cassie got to know them better, they could reassure her that she had nothing to worry about.

Now, he only had to pray it worked out that way.

"ARE WE NEARLY there?" Cassie asked for the third time in the last hour.

Quinn couldn't stop a laugh from escaping. "Soon, sweetheart. Soon."

"I'm being silly. I know I am. It's just that I can't wait to see my grandmama. It seems like it's been forever when I know it hasn't even been six months yet."

"But six months is a long time when it's someone you were used to seeing every day of your life."

"It is, isn't it?"

"Yes," he answered. "Have you thought of what you'd like to do while we're in Town?"

"I'd like to buy Molly and Lizzy some books and a new doll each."

"Very good," he answered her. "I meant for yourself. Have you thought of something you'd like to do while we're in London?"

"I would like to go to the symphony," she said. "Would you mind?"

"Of course not," he said reaching for her hand. "I enjoy the symphony as much as the next person. It will be satisfying."

"Have you thought of what *you'd* like to do?" she asked him.

"Actually, there is one thing I would like to do."

"What?"

"I would like to impose on your grandmother to host a dinner for two of my friends. I would like you to get to know them better, and I'd like to catch up on everything that's happened since we left."

"Oh, I'm sure Grandmama would enjoy getting to know your friends. She always enjoys entertaining."

"Good," he answered. "Now, get ready. We're almost there."

Cassie leaned over to look out the window. "Have you

missed London?" she asked as they entered the city.

"A little," he answered thoughtfully. "But not overly much. It's a wonderful place to visit, but I wouldn't want to live there all the time."

She smiled. "I feel the same way. I love the peace and quiet of the country, and the clean air. Everything is so fresh and open in the country compared to the smoke and the smells of city life. Grandmother always said it was impossible to smash so many people so close and still allow fresh air to get between them."

"She was right," he said as they turned a corner, and the streets became smoother and better maintained. The next street they turned down was Mayfair. It wasn't long until their carriage stopped, and Quinn got out to help Cassie to the ground.

"Grandmama!" she exclaimed rushing up the walk and into her grandmother's arms.

"Sweetling," her grandmother greeted, cupping her withered hands to Cassie's cheeks. "Lord Rosemont," she greeted Quinn, and he took her offered hand and kissed her fingers. "Come in. Oh, it's so good to have you here."

Cassie and Quinn helped the dowager into the house, then into the drawing room. Talk was non-stop from that moment on, until Quinn excused himself to go see Theo, Jack, and Secretary Waterford, his commander – the man who issued his orders.

⇒⇒⇒❯❮⇐⇐⇐

"SO TELL ME, Cassandra. How are you and the earl getting along?"

Cassie looked at her grandmother and smiled. "Oh, Grand-mama. I'm so confused."

"What is it, sweetling? Has he mistreated you? If he has—"

"No, Grandmama. He's been nothing but loving and kind."

"Then what is it?"

"Oh, Grandmama," Cassie said through her tears. "I'm afraid I've fallen in love with him, and I can't have."

The dowager countess reached out and patted her granddaughter's hand. "Whyever not? It's natural to fall in love with your husband."

"Not when your husband leaves you for weeks on end and you don't know if he's going to come back dead or alive."

"I see," her grandmother said after a long pause. "So it's not your husband you find terrifying. It's his work for the government."

"You know what he does for the government, don't you?"

"Yes, dear, I know. And it's important work. The country is much safer because of him."

"But what if he should die while on one of his missions?"

"What if hundreds of English citizens die because he *doesn't* go on one of his missions?"

"Oh, Grandmama. I'm not sure I'd survive if I lost him." Cassie swiped at a tear that spilled from her eye. "What am I going to do?"

"Only you can answer that, Cassie. Only you can decide between your own safety and the safety of your country's citizens."

"It's not fair to put it that way, Grandmama. I wouldn't want anyone to be in danger."

"Then may I suggest that you simply come to terms with what he does and pray for his safety whenever he has to go on a mission."

"That requires a great deal of faith, Grandmama. I'm not sure I have a faith that strong."

"Then perhaps that is the first thing you should ask from God, a faith that can handle anything He gives you. It's not as if He hasn't showered you with numerous blessings already. He's blessed you with a wonderful husband, two little girls to love and care for, and a home of your own.

"You're right, Grandmama. How could I not recognize all the blessings I've already received?"

"Now, tell me about your home. Have you started fixing the

interior?"

"Oh, Grandmother. I wish you could see it."

Cassie told her grandmother all of the improvements she'd already made and what she had planned. She and her grandmother visited a while longer, then Cassie realized her grandmother had tired. "Do you need to lie down for a while?"

"Yes, I believe I would like to rest a while before your husband returns. Hopefully, he'll bring his two friends with him. I'm looking forward to meeting them."

"I'm looking forward to getting to know them better, too," Cassie said, helping her grandmother to her room. She helped her lie down, then drew the counterpane around her.

Cassie was ever so glad Quinn had brought her with him and she had this chance to see her grandmother. She seemed much weaker than she'd been when Cassie had last seen her. Much more fragile.

When Cassie returned to the library, she thought of everything her grandmother had said to her. Her grandmother had only reinforced the conclusion Cassie had come to concerning Quinn's work for the government. She supported Cassie's decision that the work he did was monumental compared to the risks he took when he went on a mission. This was the first time she'd thought about the number of lives he saved and the good he did. The first time she had to face how selfish she was to want to keep him all to herself, when letting him go on the missions the government sent him on would do so much good.

She didn't have the right to keep him to herself.

Suddenly, she was aware of approaching footsteps. She looked up to find Quinn in the doorway.

"What are you doing here by yourself?" Quinn asked as he entered the room.

"I was waiting for you," she said, rising to her feet and making her way to where Quinn stood. She wrapped her arms around him and held him tight. "I've missed you."

"If this is how you greet me when you've missed me, I'll be

sure you miss me more often," he said, then leaned down and kissed her. "Is something wrong, Cassie?" he asked when he broke their kiss.

"No, everything's fine."

"Where's your grandmother?"

"She went to her room to rest for a while."

"Is she well?"

"As well as she can be," Cassie answered honestly.

Quinn nodded in understanding.

"Will your friends join us for dinner?"

"Yes. They are both eager to know you better."

"As am I."

"Would you like to rest a while before dinner?"

Cassie looked at the seductive glint in Quinn's eyes and let him lead her up the stairs.

✦

CHAPTER ELEVEN

CASSIE HADN'T ENJOYED an evening as much as she enjoyed her time with Quinn and his two friends, Theo and Jack. She couldn't have imagined any two friends more different, yet more alike.

They were both similar in stature to Quinn, with broad shoulders and a muscular build, but what was evident in the three of them was the pride they had in their country and their determination to make their world a safer place.

Cassie knew Quinn intended to steer the conversation away from politics and the events they were involved in, but as soon as the dowager countess retired for the evening, there was no hope of achieving that objective.

"Have you heard anything about what Napoleon's nephew is doing?" Theo asked taking a sip of his brandy.

Jack sat forward in his chair. "I'm afraid he's going to cause as much trouble as his uncle."

"He doesn't have the following, though," Quinn added. "Nor does he possess the military genius Napoleon I had."

"You're right," Theo agreed, "but that might make him more dangerous."

The three of them shared looks that made Cassie uncomfortable. Quinn caught her concern and tried to change the conversation.

"Perhaps we can talk about something more pleasant," he said.

"No, Quinn," Cassie interrupted. "I would like you to continue. This is something that concerns me, too."

Quinn's eyebrows rose. "But there's no need for us to bother you with what might happen in the future."

"Yet all of you are worried about it."

"We're just anticipating what might come about, and how it might affect us."

"Then I would like to know it, too," she said, placing her hand over his. She squeezed his fingers, and he returned her gesture.

"You don't have to worry about your husband, my lady," Theo said with a reassuring smile. "We're seldom sent on hazardous missions."

"That's what Quinn tells me, but it's my duty to worry about him, even though he tells me my concerns are unfounded."

Quinn's friends shared a look with him that told him they sympathized with him. He acknowledged their look by raising his glass, then taking a long swallow of his brandy. "Yes, I should have made sure the woman I married lacked the intelligence my wife has."

Cassie took a sip of her wine. "You would have been bored with a dull-witted wife within a week, my lord."

"She knows you very well already, Colonel," Jack said on a laugh.

"I'm afraid she does," Quinn agreed.

"You mentioned a Commander Waterford," Cassie said. "What exactly does he do?"

"Just what his title says, Cassie," Quinn answered her. "He is our commander. He is in charge of what missions we go on, and which one of us goes where."

"I see," Cassie said.

"Your husband is the most proficient in French," Theo said, "so if there is a mission that takes us to France, Quinn is most likely Waterford's first choice."

"What about you?" Cassie asked Theo.

"I don't have any special talents," Theo joked.

"I doubt that's true," Cassie answered.

"Theo was one of the best trackers in the regiment," Jack answered her. "If we need to find someone, he'd be the first one to be sent."

Cassie looked at Jack. "And what is your special gift?"

Quinn held up his hand when Jack started to speak. "Jack's going to tell you he had no special gifts, but he's probably the most gifted of us all. He knows more about medicine than most of the doctors in Her Majesty's service, and if any of us gets injured, he's the one we want to patch us up."

"Then I hope Jack is commanded to go with you on every mission," Cassie said.

"That would be a waste," Quinn said, reaching for Cassie's hand and squeezing her fingers. "I don't plan on needing his services. Our missions aren't that hazardous."

"That's correct, Cassie," Jack said. "What we're called on to do is a walk in Hyde Park compared to where we were sent during the war in Crimea."

"I know you are only trying to ease my mind," Cassie said.

"Is it working?" Jack asked.

"Perhaps a little," Cassie said with a smile on her face.

"Good," Quinn said, gently squeezing her fingers.

Quinn's friends stayed an hour more, then left. "Would you like to take a walk through the garden before we retire?" he asked her.

"I'd love to."

Cassie rose and Quinn led her through the French doors and out onto the terrace. The weather was perfect for a late-night stroll, and they walked down the path to the center of the garden.

"I truly like your friends, Quinn. I can see why you formed such a bond with them."

"Can you?"

Cassie smiled. "Yes. They are more similar to you than I'm sure even you realize."

"How interesting."

"Yes. I found it so, too."

"In what ways?"

"Well, in their strength of character. It's the same as yours. And their intelligence. They are very quick witted, and they have an understanding of things without having to be told."

"Oh, my," Quinn said on a chuckle. "I must make sure I don't tell them what you said. Especially Theo. Such a compliment will let his head grow even larger than it is."

"No, it won't. All three of you are quite modest concerning your abilities. That's what makes you so likable and unassuming."

Quinn stopped on the paved pathway and turned Cassie in his arms. "You're quite the find, Cassie. I don't know what I did to deserve you, but I'm grateful I found you."

"You didn't find me, Quinn. I found you. Or rather, Grandmother found you for me."

"That she did," he said, then lowered his head and pressed his lips to hers.

His kiss was passionate and filled with desire. It provided all the proof she'd ever need that...if he didn't love her, he at least cared a great deal for her.

Cassie stood on her tiptoes and wrapped her arms around his neck. She answered his desire by showing him just how much she cared for him.

One kiss led to another and before more time passed, their breathing turned heavy and labored.

"Maybe we should go in," Cassie said, lifting her mouth from his.

"Yes. That's an excellent idea."

Quinn led her inside and to their room. Once inside, he laid her on the bed and came to her.

Cassie couldn't hold him close enough, or mold her body to his as much as she desired. And she knew without a doubt that she couldn't love him more than she did at this moment. He was the only man she would ever love.

⇶❋⇷

THE WEEK WENT by too rapidly, and it was soon time to return to Rosemont. Cassie looked out the carriage window at the passing scenery and felt both regret at leaving her grandmother, and excitement at returning to her home and to Lizzy and Molly.

Quinn had allowed her several more days in London than they'd originally planned. Cassie knew part of the reason was that he realized just how ill her grandmother was. Cassie realized the same. She found leaving her more difficult this time than it had been before. This time, Cassie was certain it was the last time she'd see her grandmother alive.

"Are you all right?" Quinn asked as they traveled to Rosemont.

"Yes, I'm fine. Leaving Grandmama was more difficult because I doubt I will see her again. She was much worse, don't you think?"

"Yes," he said, then placed his hand over hers.

"Thank you for allowing me to stay with her several more days. I know that wasn't your plan."

"No, but I found it advantageous. There were several business matters I cleared up by staying longer."

Cassie looked out the window to where Theo and Jack rode at the side of the carriage. "Did your business have anything to do with why Theo and Jack are returning to Rosemont with us?"

Quinn smiled. "Perhaps."

"Can you tell me about it?"

"There's nothing to tell yet. It's just in preparation for events that might happen. If certain trips are necessary, Rosemont is a perfect location to be headquartered. I hope you don't mind them visiting."

"Not at all." Cassie gave Quinn's hand a gentle squeeze. "I like them very much and enjoy their company, as do you."

"Yes, I do. It will be good to have them with us. I've missed their company."

"Then I'm glad they will be staying with us for a while."

Quinn moved to sit beside her and wrapped his arm around her shoulders. "You look tired, Cassie. Do you feel all right?"

"I just need some sleep. Thanks to you, we didn't get much sleep last night."

Quinn pulled her closer to him and held her tight. Cassie leaned her head on his chest and let her eyes drift shut. She was on the edge of falling asleep, but it was impossible to doze when there were so many thoughts running through her mind.

She wanted to think that it was normal for the government to send the three men best suited to gathering information to a centralized location away from London, but she knew it wasn't.

The government had a specific mission they were to accomplish.

And whatever it was, Cassie knew there must be danger involved.

⟫⟫⟫⟪⟪⟪

IT WAS TOTAL chaos when they arrived at Rosemont. Both Lizzy and Molly were desperate for their attention. It was evident that both little girls had missed Quinn and Cassie, and a great party was held to present them with the gifts they'd brought back from London.

Of course there were books, and puzzles, and each got a new doll. It took hours to convince Lizzy to wait until bedtime to read one of her new books.

In time, Molly started to fuss and needed to go upstairs. Thankfully, Lizzy was content to go up with her, as long as she could take her new presents. Cassie went with them to help Miss

Portsmouth feed them dinner and get them ready for bed, while Quinn stayed below with Theo and Jack.

"You've got yourself quite the family, Colonel," Theo said, taking the snifter of brandy Quinn offered him.

"That I do." Quinn handed Luc a snifter of brandy, then sat in an empty chair next to Theo.

"I can see why you realized it was to your advantage to take a bride. *Especially* one who was financially well off, and was such a perfect match to you."

"You definitely struck gold when you found Lady Cassandra," Jack said.

"Yes, I did," Quinn agreed. "I couldn't have asked for anyone more perfect."

Quinn checked the door to make sure it was closed. "Do either of you know why it was important for you to accompany me? I take it there's a reason Commander Waterford needs the three of us at Rosemont."

Jack took another sip of his brandy then leaned forward in his chair. "All I know is that it has something to do with Rosemont's location. It will save several hours off our travel time should we have to journey to France."

"Don't tell me our government is *that* concerned Napoleon III is planning to follow in his uncle's footsteps." Quinn couldn't stop his heart from beating faster in his chest.

"One of our couriers intercepted a message he sent to the French ambassador. It's possible he's trying to gain support from loyal Frenchmen living in England," Theo answered.

Quinn tightened his grip on his brandy snifter. "Surely he isn't attempting an uprising."

"That's the question everyone is asking," Jack said.

"There are also rumors of unrest circulating," Theo said, finishing his brandy.

"What kind of unrest?" Quinn asked.

"I think that's what we're supposed to find out," Theo answered.

Quinn wanted to ask more of his friends, but the door opened. Cassie entered, and the three men rose.

"Please, remain seated," she said, then walked to the sideboard and poured herself a glass of wine.

"Did you get them settled?" Quinn asked when she sat in the chair next to him.

"Yes," she said with a smile. "But it wasn't easy. I think we overdid it with the presents, Quinn. We spoiled them worse than on Christmas."

"I'm afraid you are right," he answered.

Cassie took a sip of her wine, then stood with her glass in her hand. "I checked with Rievers, and Cook has prepared a late dinner. I'm sure you are all famished after our long day."

"That we are, my lady," Jack said, and they all rose and followed Quinn as he led Cassie from the room to the small dining room. They sat while the footmen served a hearty meal of roast beef, ham, and smoked salmon.

"I've been doing a great deal of thinking," Cassie said when they'd finished the main course, then a pudding, chocolate gateau with cream, was served.

"I can't wait to hear this revelation," Quinn said, taking a bite of his gateau.

"It's nothing earth-shattering," Cassie continued. "I just think that since the four of us will be spending a lengthy time together we should dispense with formality. My name is Cassie. It is what Quinn calls me, and I would appreciate it if you called me that, too."

"It would be our pleasure, Cassie," Theo and Jack said with smiles on their faces.

"And, please, there is no need to stand when I enter a room. You could both wear out your knees if you rise each time I enter and exit."

Quinn's friends laughed.

"If you insist," Theo said.

"I do."

"Then you must call us by our Christian names, too. Jack and Theo."

"Theo and Jack it is," she answered. "Now, I'm going to retire for the evening and leave you three to solve the world's problems. Good night," she said cheerily, then left the room.

"You have found yourself a jewel amongst women, Colonel," Theo said after the door closed and Cassie was out of hearing.

"Yes, I have. But it wasn't that long ago that I feared I would lose her."

"Why?" they both asked in confusion.

"Because of what we do. Waterford sent me on a mission I was sure would only take two, perhaps three days, but took four weeks. When I returned home, Cassie had her bags packed and was ready to leave. She told me she hadn't married me to become a widow. She said she'd rather live without me than watch me go on countless missions never knowing if I would return or not."

"Do you blame her?" Jack asked, filling their glasses with more brandy.

"We're not in near the danger we were before," Quinn said, taking a small sip of his brandy. "If Cassie knew about some of the assignments we went on during the war, she would never have married me. The missions we're sent on now are nothing compared to what we did before the war ended."

"Tell that to someone who waits day after day and night after night for their husband to come home and when they do they're in a pine box."

Quinn focused on the sober expression on Jack's face. "Is that what happened to you, Jack?" Quinn asked. All he ever knew of Jack's life was that there was someone special who had left him because of the dangers he took. And when she did, she broke his heart and left him a shell of the man he'd once been.

"That was more than two years ago. A time I prefer to forget."

"Except you haven't, have you?" Theo asked.

"Do any of us really forget? Could you forget Cassie if she left you, Colonel?"

Quinn thought about what Jack said. No, he could never forget her. Not even after he took his last breath. She would always be with him.

"Are you ever going to talk about it, Jack?" Theo asked.

"Perhaps someday. But I'll have to be a great deal more inebriated than I am tonight to tell you my sad tale."

"Then, it will have to wait for another night, I'm afraid. Finish your brandy," Quinn ordered. "We need to get to bed. I intend to give you a tour of the estate first thing in the morning. You'll need to know the area if you're going to have to make your way around it in the dark."

"You two go on up," Jack said when they'd finished their brandy. "I'm going to tour the grounds to make sure everything's secure."

"We'll see you in the morning," Quinn said, then left Jack to himself. Quinn knew his goal wasn't to check the grounds. Jack needed to walk until he could forget the woman he couldn't get out of his mind. A woman Quinn knew he'd loved and lost.

❦

CHAPTER TWELVE

CASSIE WOKE LATE the following morning and barely made it to the basin before she was sick. She waited until her stomach calmed, then dressed with Leann's help, but had to stop to rest twice before she was ready to go down to breakfast. The thought of eating anything turned her stomach more violently than it was already churning.

"Are you well, my lady?" Leann asked when Cassie sat on the nearest chair before leaving her room.

"Yes, Leann. I'm fine. Just overly tired, I think."

"Are you sure that's what it is?"

Cassie turned her gaze to where Leann stood near the door and saw the knowing in her eyes.

"No, Leann. I'm not sure that's what it is. In fact, I sincerely doubt that's what it is."

"How many courses have you missed, my lady?"

"Two. This month will be the third."

"Oh, my lady. Congratulations! This is wonderful news."

Cassie's heart jumped in her breast. "It is, isn't it?"

"Of course, it is, my lady. I can't think of anything more wonderful. Does his lordship know yet?"

Cassie shook her head. "No, and I don't want to tell him until I'm sure."

"I think you are already sure, my lady."

Cassie clasped her hands over her stomach. "Yes, I am."

"So why don't you want his lordship to know?"

"What if he's not happy about having another babe? About being responsible for another child?"

"Oh, my lady. I don't think that should concern you. His lordship was born to be a father. That's evident by how wonderful he is with the two little ones he has now."

"You're right, Leann. He's perfect with them. I'm only being silly."

"Come, my lady. You need to have something to eat whether you're hungry or not. You're eating for two now, you know."

Cassie smiled. Leann was correct. She was eating for two, and she hadn't eaten properly for days now. It was time she took better care of herself. If not for herself, then for the babe she was carrying.

That thought caused her heart to leap in her breast. *For the babe she was carrying.*

Quinn's babe.

Cassie lovingly placed her hands over her stomach. Quinn's babe was nestled there, and a smile lifted the corners of her mouth. Her heart suddenly swelled in her breast. She'd been blessed beyond belief, and she would always be thankful for the life growing inside her.

Cassie left her room and walked down the stairs. She wanted to skip into the room and shout her news to everyone in the house, but when she entered the breakfast room, it was empty.

Cassie went to the buffet and filled a plate with more food than she'd ever be able to eat. At least, she tried to eat, even though her stomach rebelled at the thought of putting food in it. She sat at the table and let a footman bring her a fresh pot of tea. She took one sip and let the warm liquid soothe her stomach.

Before she could take her first bite of toasted bread, she heard footsteps approaching. She looked up to find Quinn entering the room.

"Good morning, my lady."

"Good morning, my lord."

He smiled at her formal greeting. "You look… different this morning. As if you have just discovered a secret you swore you wouldn't tell another living soul."

"Do I?"

"Yes, you do. So, are you going to tell me what it is?"

"Yes, I think I might. But not just yet. I haven't had my breakfast yet, nor have I been to see the girls."

"They will survive without bothering you first thing in the morning."

"They're no bother and you know it."

Quinn smiled as he poured himself a cup of tea. "I can tell there's something on your mind, Cassie."

Cassie studied Quinn's expression and noticed a strange look on his face.

"Just as I can tell there's something on your mind, too, Quinn. What is it?"

He lifted his head and his grin broadened when he looked at her. "It's almost frightening how well you can read me."

"Something I will remind you of whenever you attempt to tell me something that is not quite accurate."

"I'll remember that."

"Be sure you do. Now, what is it?"

"We got a message this morning."

"Who is 'we'?"

"The three of us."

"I see."

Cassie tried to pretend that his words didn't terrify her, but they did. She tried to convince herself that what he was saying was no more serious than talk of the weather, but she couldn't. He was going to tell her that he, Theo, and Jack had gotten a message and that meant they would be sent on a mission.

Several thoughts went through Cassie's mind at the same time. She'd been through this already. She'd convinced herself that one of the reasons she loved him as desperately as she did was because of the kind of person he was. She doubted there was anyone in all of Britain who was more honorable and upstanding than Quinn. She knew that his willingness to risk his life to protect others made him the man he was.

And those were only some of the reasons she loved him like she did.

"So what did your message say?"

"We have an assignment. Theo and Jack are already packing. We'll be leaving within the hour."

"How long will you be gone this time?"

"I don't know, Cassie. I'd like to say not long, but I can't."

"Can you tell me where you're going?"

Quinn lowered his gaze to the tea cooling in his cup.

"I see." Cassie wanted to pretend it didn't matter that he was leaving before she had a chance to tell him her news, but it did matter. More than she wanted to admit. But she couldn't let him know that.

Quinn placed his hand atop hers and gently squeezed her fingers. She looked up at him and smiled.

"I'm glad you won't be going alone. I feel better that Theo and Jack will be with you."

"I thought you would," he said, rising to his feet and taking her with him. When she was standing before him, he pulled her to him and wrapped his arms around her "Do you feel well, Cassie?"

"Of course," she answered, looking up at him. "I feel fine."

"Promise me you'll get plenty of rest while I'm gone. You need to catch up on your sleep. You seem tired."

"I can assure you I'll get much more sleep when you're gone than when you are here."

"Of that I have no doubt," he said, leaning down and kissing her. "I do have a habit of keeping you awake most nights, don't I?"

"Damnable habit, yes, but I'll suffer through it," she said with a wink and an answering kiss. She dreaded to see him leave. She would miss him desperately when he was gone.

"I love you, Cassie," he said and kissed her again.

"I love you, too, Quinn. I think I always have."

Cassie thought back to the day when her grandmother told her the plan for Cassie to marry Quinn. She was *certain* she would never be able to love him. She was *sure* she could never love another man after her heart had been shattered. But somehow, she'd fallen helplessly in love with Quinn even though she tried not to. Although she was convinced she could never love another man after she'd been so embarrassed and humiliated, Quinn had stolen her heart and it would never be hers again.

Cassie lifted her gaze to look at him and reminded herself that she had to be strong. This was his work and she had to let him go.

He gave her another quick kiss on the mouth then broke away when Theo interrupted them from the doorway.

"We need to leave, Colonel."

"Coming," Quinn answered, then he kissed her on the forehead and left her.

Cassie watched from the window as the three men rode down the lane. She would like to have told him about the baby, but now wasn't the time. He had enough to think about and worry over without adding her to his concerns. And, God willing, it wasn't as if she wouldn't still be pregnant when he returned.

When the men were out of sight, Cassie went to the nursery to spend the morning with the girls. There was nothing she enjoyed more and being with them would help keep her mind from thinking of Quinn.

Cassie couldn't believe how fast they were growing. And she was always impressed by how intelligent they were. Lizzy caught on to everything Cassie taught her the first time she was told. She had a vocabulary that was remarkable for someone her age. And she was able to pick out certain words when Cassie read to her, such as *the, and, for,* and *frog.* 'Frog' came from her favorite story.

Cassie couldn't wait to see what Lizzy had to tell her today. She climbed the stairs. When she reached the nursery, she opened the door.

"Aunt Cassie, did Uncle Quinn tell you he was going on a trip?" Lizzy asked before Cassie could enter the room.

"Yes, he did."

"Did he tell you where he was going?"

"No, he didn't tell me."

"He didn't tell me, either, and I asked him two times."

Cassie sat in the nearest chair and lifted Lizzy to her lap. "What do you think it meant when your Uncle Quinn didn't answer your question the first time you asked?" Cassie asked her.

Lizzy thought for several long seconds. "Probably that he didn't want me to know."

"I think you are right. So, what should you have done instead of asking him a second time?"

Lizzy lowered her head. "I probably shouldn't have asked him again."

"That's exactly correct. But that's all right this once. I know you'll remember and never do it again."

"No, Aunt Cassie. I'll remember to only ask one time."

"Very good. Now, would you like to play a game?"

"Did you come to play with me?" she asked, jumping up and down.

"Yes, I did. With you and with Molly."

Lizzy stopped jumping. "Molly can't play yet. She's too little."

"Yes, but I can play with her."

"How?"

"Watch." Cassie walked over to the crib and picked Molly up. When she had her in her arms, she walked to a chair and sat with her in her lap.

Molly was a beautiful little girl, as was Lizzy. They both had brown curly hair and huge brown eyes. Although Lizzy's lashes were longer than Molly's, Molly's eyes were a deeper, mesmerizing brown. Cassie didn't doubt they would both be beautiful young ladies.

When Cassie had Molly settled on her lap, she reached into

her pocket and removed a pastry she'd taken from the breakfast table. She broke off a small piece and placed it in her hand. "Now watch, Lizzy. Molly and I are going to play hide-and-seek."

"Molly's too little to play hide-and-seek."

"You watch."

Cassie put the piece of pastry in her hand and Molly reached for it and gobbled it right down. Then, Cassie broke off another small piece and placed it in her hand, but this time she closed her fist. She quickly shifted the bit of pastry to her other hand and held both hands out to Molly.

Molly lifted Cassie's fingers to find the bit of pastry, but it wasn't there. She quickly lifted the fingers of Cassie's other hand and found the pastry and ate it.

Lizzy squealed with delight. "She found it!"

"Yes, she did," Cassie answered.

"Can I do it?"

"Of course, you can. You and Molly can take turns. I'll hide the pastry from you, then I'll hide it from Molly. That way you can play together."

"Oh," Lizzy squealed. "That will be fun. I can play with Molly."

"Yes, you can play with Molly. And when she gets older, there will be other games you can play together."

"Oh, that will be so much fun."

Cassie played with the girls a little while longer, then rocked Molly until she fell asleep. She couldn't believe how much she'd come to love this little family of hers. Couldn't believe how much she yearned for a family of her own, and now she'd have it.

Even though someday she'd have children of her own, she would always love Lizzy and Molly. In fact, that was how she thought of them – as if they *were* her own. And when she had the babe that was growing inside her, he would be one more child in their family.

Cassie stopped. She'd referred to the babe growing inside her as *he*. Suddenly, she knew that Quinn's babe would be a boy. She just knew it.

She looked down at little Molly sleeping in her arms and tried to imagine what her babe would look like. No doubt, he would look very similar to Molly.

Cassie held the babe until Cook's daughter brought up their luncheon, then she went to the library to work on the estate ledgers. She found she needed to keep herself busy or her mind would wander to places she didn't want it to go.

Places that were filled with worry over Quinn.

CHAPTER THIRTEEN

DAYS WENT BY in agonizing slowness as Cassie waited for Quinn to return. It had been nearly a month since Quinn, Theo, and Jack had left and there'd been no word from them, although Cassie hadn't expected there to be.

She kept herself as busy as possible. Thankfully, her morning sickness was over. Even though she was no longer ill in the mornings, there were times when her stomach was a little upset. But that didn't happen with the frequency it previously had.

What she suffered from was a lack of energy, and even a loss of weight. Although her middle was increasing, she was rarely hungry. She knew she needed to eat more, but the thought of putting food in her mouth didn't settle well. She blamed her lack of appetite on the fact that she was worried about Quinn. She was certain that as soon as he returned, her appetite would come back. As well as the color to her cheeks. Even Leann commented on her pale complexion.

She spent nearly every morning with the girls, and took Lizzy and Molly for walks in the garden. Lizzy ran ahead of her while Cassie pushed Molly in a pram. If only Quinn were home, they would have been perfect days. He would have been surprised at how much the girls had grown. Lizzy, especially, was so eager to learn that Cassie had hired a tutor to teach her French and piano. There wasn't anything she wasn't ready to absorb.

On this particular day, Cassie took the girls for a walk in the garden, then stopped when Leann came rushing to meet them.

"My lady," Leann said, nearing them almost at a run.

"What is it, Leann? Has something happened?"

"There are men coming up the lane. Three of them."

Cassie's heart leaped in her breast. Quinn was home. She couldn't be happier. She'd missed him more than she could say. She couldn't wait to go out to greet him.

"Mind the girls," Cassie ordered joyfully, then raced back to the house. As soon as she reached the library, she looked out the window and saw what Leann was telling her. Like she said, there were three men coming up the lane. But something was wrong.

Two of the men were riding horses but the third horse was riderless. Cassie looked closer. The third man was riding in front of the first rider as if he needed assistance to remain upright.

Cassie tried to make out the injured rider's identity, but it was impossible. He was slumped over enough that his face was hidden. And the other riders had thrown a large coat over him to protect him.

"Rievers," she shouted. "Ready a room and send for the doctor. Get some cloths and bandages ready."

"Yes, my lady."

Several servants rushed through the house following Cassie's orders while Cassie raced through the front doors.

She kept her gaze focused on the riders, praying that they would get close enough for her to make out their faces. Praying that the one who was injured wasn't Quinn.

She went down the steps as the horses approached and got her first clear glimpse of the riders. Jack was alone on his horse.

Cassie focused on the second rider and breathed a sigh of relief when she realized Quinn rode the second horse. Theo was the injured one barely able to stay atop his horse.

"Have you sent for the doctor, Cassie?" Quinn called.

"Yes, Quinn. He should be here shortly. And there's a room prepared for Theo!"

"Good."

Quinn slid from his horse and caught Theo as he lost his balance and fell into Quinn's arms. Jack and two footmen were there to help catch him.

"This way," Cassie said and led the way up the stairs and to the room they'd readied for Theo.

Cassie stepped back while Quinn and Jack laid Theo on the bed and removed his boots and stripped him from the waist up. That's when Cassie got a clear look at the bullet wound in Theo's chest.

"Here," Cassie said, setting a basin of water beside Quinn and a stack of cloths. "We'll need a bottle of Scotch," she ordered the nearest footman.

It only took a scant minute for him to race from the room and return with a bottle of Scotch. Cassie poured some into a glass and handed it to Quinn.

Quinn helped Theo drink, then set the glass down on the bedside table and took the damp cloth Jack handed him.

The second he pressed the cloth to Theo's upper chest, Theo jerked then let out a deep groan of pain.

"Hold him still, Jack," Quinn cautioned.

Jack anchored his arm across Theo's chest. "Catch his feet," Quinn ordered the two footmen standing at the foot of the bed. When they had Theo secured, Quinn reached for a long metal instrument, held it over the basin and doused it with whisky, then inserted it into Theo's flesh.

"Give him more whisky, Cassie."

When Theo had swallowed the whisky, Quinn began his probing again.

Huge droplets of perspiration ran down Quinn's face and Cassie cleared them with a clean cloth. Then she wiped Theo's face. When Quinn paused his probing, she let Theo drink more whisky.

Quinn swiped the perspiration from his forehead with the sleeve of his shirt, then let his gaze lock with Jack's.

"We've got to get the bullet out, Colonel," Jack said. "He's losing too much blood. We've got to get it stopped."

"Do it," Theo slurred. "Get the damn bullet out!"

"You're not the one who should have been shot, you idiot. You're the one who knows the most doctoring. Why did you step in front of me?"

"I thought you… needed the… practice digging… out a… bullet." Theo panted. "I already know how."

"Well, you're going to be sorry you let me practice on you."

Quinn swiped his sleeve over his eyes, then gripped the metal instrument and inserted it once again into Theo's flesh.

Theo released a pain-filled growl and wadded the covers in his fists as he gripped the bed coverings with all his might.

"*Bloody—*" Theo bellowed.

Quinn worked for what seemed an eternity to get the bullet from Theo's chest, but finally he was able to remove it. The second he pulled the bullet out, Cassie stood ready with the bottle of whisky and poured a great deal of it into the wound.

"Good girl," Quinn whispered from beside her.

Next, Cassie handed Quinn the salve Cook had sent up with the bandages.

"It's over now," Cassie whispered to Theo as she wiped his face with a cool, clean cloth.

Theo nodded but was unable to speak.

"The least you could have done would have been to pass out," Jack said, helping Quinn finish bandaging Theo's wound. "It would have saved you a great deal of pain."

"I'll remember that…for…next time."

"You'd better make sure there isn't a next time, Captain," Quinn said.

Cassie thought perhaps Quinn had been trying to add a bit of humor to the situation, but when she looked up at the concern on her husband's face, she realized he considered Theo's wound too serious to make light of it.

"Here, Theo," Cassie said, holding the glass of whisky to his lips. "Would you like another swallow?"

Cassie helped Theo drink, then rinsed her cloth in clean water and pressed it to his forehead.

Even with his face contorted with pain, Captain Theodore Dunworthy was a devilishly handsome man. Although his eyes were dull and glassed over with pain, they were usually a vibrant shade of deep blue. His smile, which he wore often, had placed deep creases to dent on either side of his mouth.

Cassie didn't know how Theo or Jack had managed to escape finding a bride as of yet, but then she remembered how Quinn had been trapped into marrying her. He would still be a free man if he hadn't been forced into a marriage of financial convenience. Without her and the girls in Quinn's life, these three rogues would be free to serve the Queen with no family fetters to slow them down.

Cassie stepped away from the bed, then turned when the door opened, and the doctor entered.

"What have we here?" he said, coming close to the bed.

"I'm glad you're here," Quinn said washing his hands in a basin of water. "I got the bullet out, but we'll need to do everything we can to eliminate any threat of infection."

"I'll do what I can," the doctor said, removing several jars and bottles from his bag. "Have you given him laudanum?"

Quinn shook his head. "We didn't have any. Just this." He pointed to the mostly empty bottle of Scotch.

"He drank all that?" the doctor asked wide-eyed.

"Most of it went to disinfecting the tool," Quinn replied.

The doctor poured a small amount of laudanum into Theo's glass and diluted it with a half jigger of rum he took from his bag. He held it carefully to Theo's lips. After Theo had swallowed it, the doctor removed the temporary bandage and administered a salve. "The laudanum should help him sleep for a while," the doctor said. "You can give him more when he wakes. And reapply this liberally, if you would. Three or four times a day." He laid a tin of ointment on the bedside table and picked up a wax-wrapped package. "After you clean the wound with water each day, apply this first." He opened the pack slightly and a familiar odor wafted from it.

"Why, it...it smells like my father's pipe," Cassie remarked.

The doctor chuckled. "And it should. Pipe tobacco, honey, a touch of garlic. Keeps the tissues from swelling." The doctor took more bandages out of his satchel then began working on Theo again. "I'll finish here, then leave him in your care. You know, of course, that you most likely saved this man's life." The doctor nodded to them then resumed bandaging Theo's chest.

"Thank you, doctor." Quinn turned to Jack. "Can you stay with Theo for a while? I believe Cassie is in need of a glass of wine."

"Of course. You might want to send up another bottle of whisky. Theo didn't leave much for anyone else."

Cassie couldn't help but smile. "I'll send you up something to eat, too. I know you must be hungry."

"Starving."

Cassie took Quinn's arm and walked down the stairs and to the room they referred to as the "sapphire salon", as its blue décor was quiet and calming. It was one of the smaller drawing rooms and more intimate than the others. The minute Cassie finished giving the staff orders to see to the things that needed to be done, she turned and found herself engulfed in her husband's arms.

"Oh, Cassie," Quinn said, covering her mouth with his own. "I've missed you."

"I've missed you, too," she answered and matched his kiss with a desperation equal to his.

She gathered his strong, muscular body in her arms and held him. There was something so protective in his embrace. Her heart swelled to bursting in her breast when his arms went around her and pressed her to his warm body.

He kissed her again, then led her to a cushioned wing chair and sat with her on his lap. He wrapped his arms around her and held her close. Then, he placed his finger beneath her chin and tilted her face upward until she was forced to look him in the eye.

"Now, tell me what's wrong? And I want the truth."

"Nothing is wrong, Quinn. Now that you are home safe and alive, nothing is wrong."

"No, Cassie. I said I wanted the truth. The truth," he said in a deeper, more insistent voice. "The color is gone from your face, and you look like you haven't eaten for a month or more. Twice I saw you have to steady yourself by holding on to the nearest piece of furniture. And as many times I watched you clutch your stomach as if you were in pain. Now, what is it?"

Cassie knew she couldn't lie to him. She knew he'd see through any falsehood she told him. And, she realized she didn't want to keep her news away from him.

She pushed herself to her feet and he let her go. She was grateful. She somehow couldn't tell him she was going to have his baby, not trapped in his arms like she had been.

She walked to the nearest window and looked outside.

Quinn moved up behind her. She heard his footsteps. She felt his nearness, the heat from his body. "Talk to me, Cassie." His arms came around her and locked at her waist. "Tell me what's wrong with you."

Cassie placed her fingers over his folded hands and gently pushed his hands until they rested over the slight swell of her belly. She knew the instant he realized what she was telling him. Every muscle in his body stiffened and the air caught in his throat.

"Cassie?" he said, turning her in his arms.

"I'm sorry, Quinn," she said between choked gasps. The tears she'd held at bay since she realized she was pregnant filled her eyes and spilled over her lashes. "I didn't think it would happen so soon. I know this isn't what you wanted, but—"

"Hush, sweetheart," he said and covered her mouth with his own. "Hush. Did you think I would not want a child?"

"I didn't know. I know how important your work is to you. I was afraid you might consider our baby an inconvenience. An unwanted burden."

"Any child we create could never be unwanted. Or a burden. It's only a blessing."

Cassie looked up at Quinn and searched for the truth in his gaze. "You're pleased, then?"

"I'm elated." His face lit with the joy his words conveyed. "I'm going to be a father. I'm going to have a child of my own."

"Oh, Quinn." Cassie wrapped her arms around Quinn's waist and held on to him with all her might.

"How long have you known?"

"Since right before you left."

"Why didn't you tell me?"

"I didn't want you to worry."

"Oh, you silly goose. There's not a day goes by that I don't worry about you."

Quinn placed his hand on Cassie's stomach where their baby – *his* babe was. "Is it normal for you to be this large already?" he asked.

"I don't know. I've never been pregnant before."

Quinn chuckled. "That makes two of us."

Cassie chuckled with him.

"Now," Quinn said, turning Cassie toward the door. "I'm exhausted, and you need to rest, too."

Together, they walked across the foyer and up the stairs. When they reached the top, Quinn lowered his head and kissed Cassie on the forehead. "Go lie down. I want to check on Theo first, then I'll join you."

"All right," Cassie said, then turned in the direction of her room. Before she took her first steps away from him, Quinn caught her hand and pulled her back.

"I love you, Cassie."

"And I love you."

As he drew away their linked hands parted, but the feel of him remained. Sure, staid, strong, and loving in the kindest, dearest way possible.

Chapter Fourteen

DAYS WENT BY in agonizing slowness. More than once Cassie was afraid they would lose Theo. The bullet wound developed an infection that seemed to take forever to heal. A fever overtook him and refused to let go. But finally, after a terrifying month, he began to improve.

"Would you like to escape the house for a while, Theo? Sit outside?" Cassie asked. "I think the fresh air would do you good."

"I'd like nothing more," Theo answered and struggled to his feet.

Cassie called for a footman and together they helped their patient down the stairs. When they reached the foyer, Quinn appeared to lead Theo to the terrace.

"Can we walk through the garden?" Theo asked.

"Not today," Cassie answered. "Sitting on the terrace will be exertion enough for your first time out-of-doors."

Theo sank into a wrought-iron chair on the terrace and stretched his legs out before him. "Is your wife always so prone to giving orders?" he asked Quinn.

"Oh, this is one of her good days," Quinn answered his friend. "You should see her when she's in one of her protective moods."

Cassie took the blanket one of the maids handed her and threw it over Theo's lap with a chuckle, then poured the tea another maid brought out.

"Oh, this is perfect," Theo said taking a sip of his tea.

"You've had a rough time of it," Quinn said, relaxing in his chair.

"I doubt I would have made it without your wife's tender care. I owe you both a great debt."

"You would have made it," Cassie said. "You're strong. Besides, we refused to let you leave us."

"That's right," Quinn said coming around the table and sitting next to Theo. "I'll need you here to help me when Cassie has her babe."

"I will be. I doubt Waterford will give me an assignment for months yet."

"I doubt he will either. I'm sure Jack will tell him you can't go anywhere for a long time yet."

"You're probably right," Theo said. "Have you had word from Jack?"

"He's in London."

"Is Napoleon III still on a rampage?"

"Yes. To make things worse, there was an attempt on his life and he's talking war against Austria in order to expel the rebels from Italy."

"Things are escalating, then?" Theo asked.

"It seems so," Quinn answered just as Cassie's babe leaped inside her. She clutched at her stomach and held it tight. Such talk did no good. It only made her fear for Quinn's future and her own.

"Are you all right?" Quinn asked.

"Yes, fine. The baby just kicked."

"Are you sure you are not going to present your husband with more than one child?" Theo asked.

"Oh, don't even suggest such a thing," Quinn said. "Caring for one babe along with Molly and Lizzy is one thing. But caring for two would be a nightmare."

Theo laughed, but Cassie couldn't help but notice the expression on Quinn's face. He may claim to be pleased about the babe

Cassie was carrying, but the look on his face, as well as the words he spoke said something different.

She suddenly felt the need to escape Quinn's watchful eye. "I think I'll rest for a while," she said as she rose. "I'll let you entertain Theo. Only don't let him stay out-of-doors too long."

Quinn got to his feet and accompanied her to the house. He wrapped his arm around her waist and held her close. "Are you sure you're all right?" he whispered in her ear.

"I'm fine," Cassie answered, putting a smile on her face. But she wasn't sure she was fine. She was as big as a stable and did not have enough energy to get through a day without resting once or twice. She even found it difficult to walk the length of the house or climb the flight of stairs to reach the nursery, but she still had nearly two months until her baby would arrive.

"Don't worry, Quinn. Everything is fine."

"You are sure?"

Cassie stood on her tiptoes and pressed her lips to his. "I am positive. I would let you know if it weren't."

"I think I'll contact Dr. Downey."

"You will do nothing of the sort. He has many other patients who need him without taking time from his busy day to babysit the wife of an anxious husband."

"But—"

"*But,* nothing, Quinn. I am perfectly fine."

"If you say so," he said kissing her before leaving to return to Theo.

Cassie couldn't erase the worried expression on Quinn's face. She had to do whatever she could to convince him that there was nothing wrong. She was just tired. That was all. That's what she prayed was the problem.

"I THOUGHT JACK would be back by now," Theo said as he and

Quinn walked the garden.

Theo was improving every day. He was far out of danger and Quinn was thankful. There were more days than Quinn wanted to remember when Quinn thought they were going to lose Theo. Day after day he was out of his mind with a raging fever. Quinn and Cassie did everything they could think of to bring his fever down, but nothing helped. Finally, it broke and for the first time in longer than Quinn could remember, he cried.

Theo was on the verge of death and Quinn didn't want to think of going on the next mission without him. He and Jack had been the best friends Quinn had ever had. Together they were like three legs of a stool. Together they were solid. With one leg missing, the other two couldn't stand.

"Did Jack say where he thought Waterford was sending him?" Quinn asked.

"No, he had no idea. He wasn't even sure there was a mission. He thought Waterford might simply want him to come to London to strategize."

Quinn considered that possibility. They'd gone weeks without an assignment, and he doubted it would be much longer before they'd have to leave again. Quinn didn't want to think that he might have to leave Cassie any day now. Not before the baby arrived.

"I'm sure he'll be back soon," Quinn said, hoping he was correct.

"Don't worry, Colonel," Theo said with a smile.

"I'm not worried. When have you known me to worry about Jack?"

"You worried about all of us, and you have that same concerned look on your face that you had after every battle we fought while you waited for your men to return. You were like a mother hen counting her chicks."

"I was not," Quinn started to say, but was interrupted by Jack's voice.

"Yes you were, Colonel," Jack said coming toward them.

"Jack!"

Quinn wrapped his friend in a huge bear-hug. "What took you so long?"

"I had to deliver a message to Waterford before I could return. And how are you doing?" he asked Theo. "You look a hell of a lot better than you did the last time I saw you."

"I feel a hell of a lot better, too."

"Come," Quinn said. "Let's go inside. You look like you could use a stiff drink and some food."

"And a good night's sleep," Theo added.

"You're right about all of it. But I'll take that drink first."

"Come," Quinn said and led his friends inside.

"What news is there?" Quinn asked when they reached his study and he'd poured everyone a drink.

"I'm afraid I've come with bad news."

"Napoleon?"

Jack shook his head. "Hopefully, we've settled that crisis. This is something more personal. This concerns your wife's grandmother. Her funeral was a few days ago."

A knot settled in Quinn's stomach. This was the last news Cassie needed to hear right now. And damn her worthless uncles for not letting her know. They had probably dismantled the poor woman's estate by now.

"I've brought a letter from the dowager countess that she wanted your wife to have," Jack said, handing Quinn a missive.

Quinn took the letter. "Thanks, Jack." He rose. "I'll have your dinner readied. Eat without me. I'll be down after I've given Cassie the news."

Quinn dreaded what he had to do. He knew Cassie would take her grandmother's death hard, but she had to be told. The sooner she heard the news, the sooner she'd recover from it. The sooner the healing process would begin.

The knot inside his stomach grew more painful with each step he took. He didn't want to cause Cassie more hurt than she'd already suffered. She wasn't well. This baby was causing her a great deal of discomfort. What if the shock of her grandmother's death was too much for her to handle? What if she wasn't able to deal with more worry and pain? What if…?

A thought raced through him that he quickly brushed away. What if this—compounded by the birth of their babe—was too much for her to handle? What if he lost her?

He stumbled on the top step and careened into the wall.

"No," he muttered beneath his breath. *No.* He couldn't survive if something happened to her. He couldn't continue without her. She was too important to him. He'd come to love her too much to lose her.

Quinn brushed such thoughts from his mind. He wouldn't lose her. God would not do something so horrible to him. He wouldn't take her away from him now that he'd found her.

"Dear God," he whispered. "Keep her safe. Don't let anything happen to her. Please. In your name I pray. Amen."

He reached Cassie's door and turned the knob. He quietly entered her room and walked to the bed.

Cassie lay beneath the covers fast asleep. He didn't want to wake her, so he gingerly sat on the edge of the bed and watched her sleep.

Her complexion had no color, and she looked terribly uncomfortable. He had no idea how large a pregnant woman was before she gave birth, but Cassie was very large. Theo asked her constantly if she was sure she was only having one baby. He teased her that he thought there were at least half a dozen babies hidden in her stomach.

Of course she denied it, but even Quinn wondered if there might be more than just one babe inside her. For such a small woman, she was huge. Quinn had to help her stand and get out of bed in the morning. He couldn't remember the last time she'd been able to see her feet. It had been months ago.

He brought the cover up around her shoulders and for several moments, she didn't realize he was there, but when he gently placed his hand on her shoulder, she stirred, then slowly opened her eyes.

"Quinn?"

"Yes, sweetheart."

"I think I was sleeping."

"Yes, you were."

"I'm sorry. I'm not a very good hostess, am I?"

"You're a wonderful hostess. You've allowed Jack and Theo and me time to talk. There's much to catch up on."

"Has Jack returned?"

"Yes, a short time ago."

Cassie attempted to rise to her feet, but Quinn stopped her from getting up. "I need to arrange for some food for him, and the staff to freshen his room."

"You need to stay laying. I've already taken care of everything."

Cassie lifted her gaze and studied him. "Is something wrong?" she asked, cupping her hand to his cheek.

"I have difficult news for you, Cassie."

"Help me sit, Quinn."

Quinn helped her sit on the edge of the bed, then he wrapped his arm around her shoulders and held her.

"What is it?"

He brought her a little closer to him. "It's your grandmother, Cassie. She's gone."

Cassie lifted her gaze and her eyes filled with tears that spilled over her lashes and trickled down her cheeks. She jerked in his arms, then clutched at her stomach.

"Are you all right?"

"Yes, Quinn. Your son is simply telling me he knows I'm sad."

"You know you're having a boy?"

"Of course. If I were having a girl, she wouldn't be nearly as rambunctious. I need to warn you. He is going to be a handful. I will have to rely on you to help me with him."

"Of course, my love."

Cassie leaned her head against his chest. "I'm glad I got to see her that last time, Quinn. Thank you for taking me to London."

"I'm glad I got to see her, too. She was a special lady."

"Yes, she was," Cassie said as she leaned against her husband and let the tears flow.

She suddenly felt very tired. Very weak.

CHAPTER FIFTEEN

QUINN STAYED WITH Cassie throughout the night. He held her close to him when her silent sobs shook her body. He caressed her back and her enormous stomach where his child nestled inside her. And he whispered that he loved her whenever he thought she was awake enough to hear him. And even when she wasn't.

Finally, the sky lightened, and she stirred.

"How do you feel, sweetheart?"

"I'm fine, Quinn."

"You don't look fine, Cassie. You look like you're in pain."

"No. I'm only uncomfortable."

Then, I'm going to take care of you today. I'm going to call for Leann to help you change into something more comfortable, then I'm going to bring you up some hot chocolate and toasted bread. Then, you're going to spend the day in bed."

"Oh, I can't," Cassie said.

"You can, and you will. After you eat, you will take a nap. Then, when you wake, I'll have Miss Portsmouth bring the girls in to see you."

"Oh, yes. I would love to see them."

"Then, when they leave, I'll come to sit with you. We'll plan a private dinner. Just the two of us."

Cassie looked at him and smiled. "That will be the highlight of my day."

"Now, I'm going to get Leann. She'll help you get comfortable, then put you back to bed. I'll return in a little while with something to eat."

Quinn leaned down to kiss Cassie, then left the room. He talked to Leann, then went down to get Cassie something to eat.

"How is she?" Theo asked when Quinn entered the bedroom.

"She's fine, although I insisted that she remain in bed. She can barely walk without running out of breath." Quinn sat down and poured himself a cup of coffee. "I'm worried about her," he told his two friends. "She's terribly uncomfortable. I'm afraid something is wrong."

"All women are uncomfortable just before they give birth," Theo said.

"How would you know?" Jack asked.

"I know because our neighbor, Mrs. Wimple, had nine children and every time she was close to birthing her babe she'd come over and tell my ma she was so uncomfortable she couldn't wait to get that babe out of her."

"All I can say," Jack said, "is that I'm damn glad it's the women who have the babes. I'm not sure I'm brave enough to go through that much pain."

Quinn finished his coffee, then filled a plate to take to Cassie. He knew he'd given her too much, but she needed to eat to keep up her strength.

He took her breakfast up to her, then sat with her while she ate. When she'd eaten as much as she could, he left her to sleep.

The girls entertained her later that day, then he sat with her for a while until Leann brought dinner to them. After they ate, Quinn went below to spend a little while with Jack and Theo, but he didn't stay long. He was desperate to return to Cassie. Something inside him told him it was important that he spend as much time with her as possible, in case...

Well, just in case.

THE SUN HAD been up nearly an hour before Cassie woke. She opened her eyes and her gaze locked with his.

"Good morning, sweetheart," he said, kissing her on the cheek. "How do you feel?"

"Like I've slept a solid twenty-four hours."

Quinn laughed. "Not quite, sweetheart. But close. Can I do anything for you?"

"My back hurts. I think it's from laying too long. Would you rub it a little?"

"Of course."

Quinn placed his hand against the small of her back and began to gently circle. She was as tense as a taut bow.

"I think I would like to get up now. I've been in bed long enough. I would like to sit in the sun for a while. Would you help me outside?"

Quinn helped her out of bed, then Leann came in and helped her put on one of the only gowns she said were large enough to fit her. When she was dressed, Quinn helped her downstairs.

"Bring your mistress a tea tray and some pastries," Quinn ordered Leann when they were out on the terrace. Leann left to get the tea and Quinn helped Cassie down the three steps to the pebbled path that led through the garden.

"Hold on to me, Cassie," he said when he felt her stagger on the path. "We won't walk long. Just to the first flowerbed."

"Can you believe I can only walk a short distance? I used to bring the girls out here all the time and chase Lizzy when she skipped down the path."

"You will again," Quinn said with a smile on his face. "Once this little one you're carrying starts walking, you'll get all the running you can manage."

"I feel like he's going to be born ready to walk."

Quinn laughed. "Let's turn around now and go back to the

house."

"Yes, let's do," Cassie agreed. They took about three steps toward the house and Cassie released an agonizing moan and doubled over in pain.

"Cassie?"

"I need to go inside, Quinn. *Oh…*" she moaned.

Without a word, Quinn scooped her up and carried her to the house. "Fetch the doctor," he ordered when they reached the bedroom.

"Yes, my lord," Leann said, then raced out of the room to send a footman for the doctor.

"Don't leave me, Quinn. Please, don't leave me."

"I won't, Cassie. I won't."

Before Quinn could issue more words of reassurance, another stabbing pain caused her to double over. She cried out in pain, then grabbed his hand in a death-like grip.

"Hang on, Cassie. The baby is ready to come."

No sooner had Quinn uttered those words than Cassie released a heart-wrenching cry.

"Where is that doctor?" Quinn bellowed.

"He's coming," Leann said. "A footman is bringing him."

"He needs to hurry."

"Quinn?" Cassie said between stabs of pain.

"What is it, sweetheart?"

"You must have patience. These things often take a great deal of time."

"I know, darling. It's only that I hate to see you suffer."

"I've never heard of a mother birthing a babe without there being a great deal of pain involved.

Cassie smiled, but the smile did not reach her eyes. She was in too much pain. Quinn could tell.

"The doctor is here," Leann announced from the doorway.

"See, Quinn," Cassie said. "There's nothing to worry about."

"How do you fare, my lady?" the doctor said taking her hand when he reached her bed.

"The same as all women when they are about to give birth."

The doctor laughed. "Yes, my lady. But do not worry. It will soon be over." The doctor turned toward Quinn. "And you, my lord, will be more help to your wife and to me if you go down and sit with your friends."

"You will call me if you should need me, won't you?"

"Of course, my lord. Now, leave your wife so she can concentrate on birthing your child."

Quinn stepped close to Cassie and kissed her cheek. "I love you, sweetheart. I'll be right here should you need me."

"I know, Quinn. I love you, too."

Quinn kissed her again, then left the room. He'd barely reached the stairway when he heard Cassie's next painful cry. He wasn't sure how he could endure listening to her cries of pain. He would suffer it all in her place if he could. He was used to pain. He'd suffered many times and knew he was strong enough to survive. But he wasn't sure he would be strong enough to survive the pain if something happened to her.

In fact, he wasn't sure he could go on even one day if she wasn't with him.

⫸⫷

He stepped into his study where Theo and Jack waited for him.

"So," Theo said. "You're about to have a child. What does Cassie say it is?"

Quinn filled a tumbler with brandy. "She's convinced it's a boy," he said, taking a sip. He wanted to drain the liquor from his glass, but he knew this would be a long day and didn't want to greet his new baby in his cups.

"And what do you say it is?" Jack asked.

"From the size of her, I'm afraid Cassie intends to present me with an entire regiment."

Both Jack and Theo laughed, then held up their glasses in a

toast.

"How long does this take?" Quinn asked. "Do either of you know?"

Jack shook his head.

"Theo?" Quinn asked. "Do you know?"

"Like I said, our neighbor woman had nine and my mom helped deliver most of them. Sometimes it didn't take long at all to have her babes. Sometimes a couple of hours or so, and other times all day."

"All day?" Jack said.

"Bloody hell!" Quinn said. "I don't think I can stand for Cassie to be in pain that long."

"We'll pray the babe comes quickly," Theo said. "Cassie is strong. I'm sure she'll have your babe in no time."

Quinn hoped she would, too. But one hour stretched to two, and two to four. And four to eight, and there was still no babe. The only activity was the constant scurrying of servants running up and down the stairs taking up stacks of clean cloths, and taking down bloody ones. Servants rushing up with basins of clean water and rushing down with bloody water.

And still Cassie's painful cries tore at Quinn's gut.

Sometime around midnight, Leann came down.

Quinn rushed to where Leann stood in the doorway. "How is she?"

"The birth is not easy, my lord. She is having a difficult time. She's lost a great deal of blood."

Quinn's knees buckled beneath him, and he reached out to steady himself against the door frame. "What can I do?"

Leann shook her head. "There's nothing anyone can do, my lord. The lady is in God's hands now."

Quinn felt as if someone had squeezed the air from him. As the air left his lungs his legs became so weak he could barely stand on them. A fear unlike anything he'd ever felt before consumed him and he couldn't take in a breath. He pushed himself through the doorway and raced up the stairs, taking the steps two at a time.

He burst through the door and raced to the bed.

"Cassie?" he said, taking her hand.

"My lord, you shouldn't be here," the doctor warned.

"Don't!" Quinn admonished.

Quinn looked down at his wife. Her face was as pale as the white gown she wore and was covered with rivers of perspiration that streamed down her forehead and cheeks. She looked practically lifeless, and Quinn couldn't bear to see her so close to death.

"Quinn?"

"Yes, sweetheart. I'm here."

"I'm glad. I want you…to know how much…I love…you."

"I know you do, Cassie. As I love you. But you can tell me later. There'll be time later."

"No, Quinn. I'm afraid…there won't."

"Don't talk like that. I won't allow it. You can't leave me."

"I'm afraid…that decision…isn't up to…me."

"No, Cassie. God won't allow you to leave me. He knows I couldn't get along without you. He knows I would be nothing without you at my side."

"Quinn?"

"Yes."

Before Cassie could utter another word, a spasm caused her to squeeze his hand in pain. Her grip was weak, trembling.

"My lady," the doctor said. "Push."

"I can't."

"You can," Quinn ordered. "I demand to see my child. Don't keep him from me."

"No…I…"

"Now!" Quinn insisted.

Cassie blinked twice, took as full a breath as her condition allowed, and cried out as she brought forth her first child.

"It's a boy," the doctor said as he took the babe, cut the cord, and handed the babe to a maid to wrap in a warm blanket.

"A boy, Cassie."

"Yes, Quinn. I knew it was a—*oh!*" Cassie cried out again.

"What is it, sweetheart? What's wrong?"

"Push, my lady," the doctor demanded.

Cassie issued a pain-filled cry as her second babe was born.

"You have another boy, my lady."

"Oh, sweetheart," Quinn said, staring in disbelief as the doctor took care of another baby, then handed the crying infant to a second maid standing by with another warm blanket.

"We have twins, Cassie. Twin boys."

Quinn wiped Cassie's face with a damp cloth. Her eyes were closed, and she looked as if she was on the verge of going to sleep. Except the look was more like she was giving up.

"Don't let her go to sleep," the doctor ordered. "Keep her awake. Keep her talking."

"Cassie? Stay awake. Do you hear me?"

"I'm tired, Quinn. So tired."

"No. The doctor says you have to stay awake."

"No," she said, barely above a whisper.

Quinn leaned closer to his wife and spoke to her. "Cassie, stay with me, sweetheart. Don't go to sleep. Don't leave me."

Quinn looked at the doctor and was met with a severe look of concern.

"I believe she's carrying another babe, my lord. And we must remove it as quickly as possible. She's lost too much blood already, and if she doesn't have the babe soon, we'll lose it. And her."

"Cassie, did you hear the doctor? He thinks you're carrying another babe. You have to be strong. You can't go to sleep yet. The babe has to be born first. Can you help me?"

"I can't…Quinn. I'm so…tired. I want to…sleep."

"No, Cassie. No! You can't sleep. You can't leave me. Do you hear me? Don't give up. Stay with me. We have a family to raise. Our babies need a mother."

"Quinn? I can't."

"You can. I need you. I can't do this alone, Cassie. Help me."

"Push, my lady. Your baby wants to be born."

"Push, Cassie," Quinn begged through the tears rolling down his cheeks. "Stay with me!"

But she started to pull away from him. He knew it. He could feel it. She was leaving him, and he knew if he allowed her to go, he'd never get her back.

"No, Cassie! No! Stay with me. Open your eyes and look at me! I need you. I can't survive without you."

"You have to push, my lady," the doctor demanded.

"I can't. I…I'm too tired."

"Just once more. Please, love. Hold on to my hand and I'll help you."

Quinn placed her hand in his. Her grip was weak. Very weak. Too weak.

"Now, push, my lady," the doctor urged again.

Quinn felt the pressure as Cassie struggled to find the strength to bring her last baby into the world. "Please, Cassie. You can do this."

"I'm…tired…Quinn. I want to…sleep."

"No, sweetheart. In a bit you can sleep, but not yet. Push once more."

At that moment, Cassie moaned the most painful moan Quinn had heard from her all day.

"Quinn!" she cried.

"Push, Cassie."

And the third baby was born into the world.

"You have another son, my lord," the doctor said, working to clean the baby and hand the squalling infant to a maid. "Three small, yet healthy sons."

"Did you hear, Cassie? There are three of them. Three!"

Quinn knelt at Cassie's bedside and brought her fingers to his lips. He kissed each hand while tears of joy ran down his face. "Do you know how much I love you, sweetheart? More than life itself."

"Would you like to see your babes, my lady?" the doctor asked.

"Yes. I want to see them."

Leann stepped to the side of the bed and placed the first babe in her arms. "Oh, look, Quinn. He has your dark hair. And a lot of it."

Quinn tried to stop the tears from rolling down his face but couldn't. He was looking at his son, his heir.

"What should we call him?" Cassie asked cradling the babe in her arms.

"Edward," Quinn answered. "After my father. Edward Jules."

"I like that," Cassie said on a sigh.

"Yes," Quinn said, then stepped to the side as a maid leaned forward and placed the second babe in Cassie's arms.

"Oh, Quinn. Look, he's almost identical to Edward, except this one has a wider nose. And his ears are flatter to his head."

"Yes, but he has my dark hair, just like his brother."

"What should we call him?" Cassie asked.

"What would you like to name him, Cassie? You can name this one."

"I think I'd like to call him Winston, after my father, and Matthew, after my grandfather."

"Winston Matthew," Quinn said. "I like it. It's a strong name. He will be a strong man when he grows up."

Then, a maid brought over the third baby and handed him to Quinn. "I'm out of arms," Cassie said.

Quinn laughed. "So you are."

"What should we name our third son, my lord?"

Quinn studied the small babe in his arms. "His hair isn't as dark as the other two, and he has dimples in his cheeks. I fear this one is going to give us trouble with the ladies, Wife. He's going to grow up to be too handsome for his own good."

"That will be your problem to handle. I am only responsible for teaching our sons to have good manners and speak politely. How they act will be your responsibility."

"That hardly seems fair, Cassie."

"Oh, it's more than fair. I birthed them and you can raise them."

"Well, if I am in charge of his discipline, then I will call my little troublemaker, Franklin. Franklin James."

"I like that. Franklin sounds like someone worthy of redemption. I believe our Franklin will not give us any trouble at all."

Quinn looked from the first son, to the second son, to the third son. They all looked so much alike. He didn't know how he would ever be able to tell them apart. He would have to pin their names on their shirts until they were at least five years old."

"Edward Jules," he said, looking at the son born first. "Winston Matthew," he said, shifting his gaze to his second son. "And Franklin James," he said looking at the babe in his arms.

"Thank you, Cassie. You have made me the happiest man alive. I am blessed more than I have a right to be blessed. And I love you more than I thought I could love anyone."

Quinn leaned down and kissed his wife. His heart swelled in his chest until he thought it might burst.

"Can I rest now, Quinn?" Cassie asked when their babes had been taken to be clothed and fed.

"Yes, darling. You can rest as long as you want."

Quinn looked down at his wife and realized how much he loved her. He couldn't fathom what he would do if he lost her.

If there was one thing he knew for sure, it was that he couldn't go on if she wasn't in his world. Or if she wasn't around for his three sons when they were growing. And their two daughters. His family was suddenly the most important thing in the world to him.

"My lord," the doctor said, interrupting Quinn from his thoughts. "Why don't you go down to share your amazing news with your friends while I take care of your wife?"

"Oh," Quinn answered. "Yes. Yes."

Quinn reached for Cassie's hand then leaned across the bed and kissed her on the cheek. "I won't go far. The doctor will call for me when you're ready."

"That's fine, Quinn. I'll be fine until you get back."

"I know you will. You're the strongest person I know."

Quinn walked to the door, then turned back before he left the room. "I love you," he whispered before he left. But Cassie had already fallen asleep.

Quinn closed the door behind him, then stood with his back against the wall. He had a big decision to make. A very weighty decision. But deep inside him he already knew what his decision would be.

⋙✦⋘

QUINN DESCENDED THE stairs on legs that threatened to collapse beneath him. He tried to absorb everything that had occurred today, but today's events seemed surreal. His mind was unable to process the magnitude of what had happened.

He was the father of three sons.

He'd nearly lost Cassie giving birth to his babes.

He gripped the railing tighter with each step he took. When he reached the bottom of the staircase, no matter how hard he tried, he wasn't able to move.

"Quinn?"

He lifted his head to see Jack and Theo staring at him with confused expressions on their faces.

"Is everything all right?" Jack asked.

Quinn tried to speak, but no words would come out. Instead, he turned around and took the first step to return up the stairs again.

He wasn't able to move with any speed, but he knew Jack and Theo followed him.

"Is Cassie all right?" Theo asked.

"Yes," he muttered.

"Is it your babe? Is something wrong with the babe?"

Quinn stopped with his hand on the bedroom door where they'd taken his babes so Cassie could get some rest. He nodded in answer to Jack's question then opened the door. He stepped inside and walked to the first cradle.

Jack and Theo followed him. They stared at the three cradles, then turned their heads and stared at him with shocked expressions on their faces.

"Bloody hell," Theo said in a choked voice.

"Are these all yours?" Jack asked, looking from one crib to the next.

"This one is Edward Jules. He was born first. This is his brother, Winston Matthew. He was born second. And, his other brother, Franklin James. He came last."

"Can you tell them apart?" Theo asked.

Quinn shook his head. "No." He reached down and brought out Edward's tiny foot. There was a leather strap tied around his ankle. "Edward has one leather strap around his ankle. Winston has two, and Franklin has three. I'm having bands made with the numbers one, two, and three emblazed on them so we never confuse them."

"Oh, Quinn," Jack said in confusion. This is unreal."

"Yes, it is," Quinn answered, then led the way out of the room when Franklin started to cry. It wasn't long before Edward and Winston joined in, and the wet nurses came in to feed the babes.

"I need something strong to drink," Quinn said when they reached the blue room.

"I can imagine you do," Theo said. "And my guess is that there will be many days when you'll need a strong drink or two."

His friends laughed at Theo's joke, but Quinn knew he was more right than not. He feared he might become a drunkard before his three sons reached their first birthday.

He tipped his glass and drained it in one swallow.

CHAPTER SIXTEEN

QUINN ENTERED HIS study and closed the door behind him. It had been one week since his three sons had been born.

Before he greeted Theo and Jack, he poured himself a glass of brandy and took a long swallow.

"Well, Colonel. Gone are your days of enjoying the peace and quiet of country life," Theo said when Quinn sat in his favorite wing chair before the fire. Theo sat on one side of him, and Jack completed the semi-circle on the other.

"I think you're right," Quinn agreed.

"Can you believe it?" Jack asked. "I mean, it's been a whole week now. Does it finally seem real?"

Quinn took another swallow of his brandy and shook his head. "I'm not sure it will ever seem real. Do you even know a family who has triplets?"

Theo and Jack shook their heads. "I've heard it was possible, but I never thought I'd see such a thing."

"Me either," Quinn said. "It's amazing. And they look so similar I'm not sure I'll ever be able to tell them apart. Although Cassie says she can."

"Of course," Jack said. "She's their mother."

"Well, I'm their father. I should be able to tell them apart, and I can't."

"You will, Colonel. Just give yourself another week or so,"

Theo said, finishing off his brandy.

"So, what are you going to do, Quinn? Have you thought any more about your future?"

Quinn leaned forward in his chair and rested his forearms on his knees. "I don't see how I can go back," he said, staring at the flames sputtering in the grate. "I'm not sure I want to. I've got too much to keep me here. Too much responsibility."

"What does Cassie say?" Theo asked.

The door opened and Cassie stood there.

"I say I'd rather have my husband happy doing what he really wants to do than doing what he thinks he's obligated to do because he's responsible for me and the children."

Quinn bolted to his feet and sped to where Cassie stood. "What are you doing out of bed? You should be resting."

Quinn wrapped his arm around Cassie's waist and led her to his chair in front of the fire.

"I've rested long enough. I need to be out of bed and be useful."

"And how do you expect to be useful?"

Cassie smiled, then looked from Jack to Theo. "By entertaining our guests."

"How are the new additions to your family, my lady?" Theo asked.

"Loud, like their father."

Everyone laughed.

"I'm not loud, Wife."

"Of course not," Cassie said in feigned agreement. "I'm sure I do not know how I came to that conclusion."

Before more could be said, a maid brought in a tea tray of fruit and pastries, which began to disappear rapidly.

"In all honesty," Theo said, after taking a bite of his pastry. "You have given your husband three fine sons, my lady."

"I couldn't agree more," Jack chimed.

"Thank you," Cassie said. "Every time I look at them I realize what a miracle they are."

"We have been given something quite spectacular," Quinn said, reaching for Cassie's hand and holding it.

"Yes, we have," Cassie answered. "Now, what is this you were telling Jack and Theo? That you are considering resigning your work with the government?"

"Things have changed, Cassie. I'm not sure I want to leave them for weeks at a time. Have you noticed how much they change just overnight? Edward seems to have doubled his weight in just one week. Just imagine how much he might change in a month, and I could miss it if Waterford sent me on an assignment."

"They are changing quite rapidly," Cassie said.

"I can't tell them apart now," Quinn said in frustration. "What will it be like if I'm gone for weeks at a time? I might never be able to tell them apart."

"That won't happen, Quinn," Cassie assured him, but Quinn didn't want to take the chance that he was gone so often that he couldn't tell his own children apart.

Jack and Theo laughed heartily at the idea of a father not being able to recognize his own children, but the serious expression on their faces told Quinn that they knew he was serious about leaving, and there was nothing they could say to change his mind.

Quinn and his friends chatted a while longer, then he looked at Cassie and was desperate to have her to himself for a while. "Would you like to take a short walk through the garden before you go back to rest?"

"I'd love to," she said, and Quinn helped his wife to her feet and escorted her to the garden.

"We'll walk to the first bench, and sit for a while," he said.

"Good. I want to talk to you."

"About what, sweetheart?" he said when they reached the first bench along the path.

"About what you said to Theo and Jack about quitting the work you do for the government."

"I meant what I said, Cassie. I have other obligations now that take precedence over anything else."

"No, you don't, Quinn. The work you do for the government is too important to give up."

Quinn wrapped his arm around Cassie's shoulders. "Do you remember what you said to me when I returned from my first mission after we were married?"

Cassie lowered her gaze to her clasped fingers in her lap. She remembered. Quinn knew she did.

"You said you didn't marry me and start to love me so I could die and leave you alone. You told me you had fallen in love with me and couldn't bear the thought of having to live your life without me."

"That was before I realized the importance of the work you did for our country."

"Be that as it may, the tables have turned. I am the one who cannot bear the thought of dying when I have so much to live for. I don't want to risk losing one day of being with you. Or our family."

"But what about your work? Who will take your place?"

"Theo and Jack will step up. If they ever need my help, I'll be here to help them, but I have five children who need me more than anyone else."

"Oh, Quinn."

Tears filled Cassie's eyes, and he brought her to him and held her close. "My children only have one father, whereas my country has many capable men who can do my job equally as well as I can."

Cassie lifted her hand and cupped her palm to his cheek, then brought his lips down to touch hers.

Quinn wrapped her in his arms and kissed her with the tenderness he felt to show her how much he loved her. God had indeed blessed him, and he would take full advantage of these blessings.

He'd spent most of his adult life engaged in espionage. Seeing his way through a dilemma had become second nature to him. Now it stunned him to realize how long it had taken him to see the dilemma he'd created in his own home.

But no longer. His heart was fixed on one thing only—family. Without them he had nothing. With them, he had a love for all time.

About the Author

Laura Landon taught high school for ten years before leaving the classroom to open her own ice-cream shop. As much as she loved serving up sundaes and malts from behind the counter, she closed up shop after penning her first novel. Now she spends nearly every waking minute writing, guiding her heroes and heroines to find their happily ever afters.

She is the author of more than a dozen historical novels, including SILENT REVENGE, INTIMATE DECEPTION, and her newest Montlake Romance release, INTIMATE SURRENDER.

Her books are enjoyed by readers around the world.